THE PRINCE'S TUTOR

NICOLE BURNHAM

The Prince's Tutor

by Nicole Burnham

Cover design by Patricia Schmitt

Edition: April 2020

ISBN: 978-1-941828-45-8 (paperback)

ISBN: 978-1-941828-44-1 (ebook)

ISBN: 978-1-941828-46-5 (audio)

For more information or to subscribe to Nicole's newsletter, visit nicoleburnham.com.

CHAPTER 1

"*Mi scusi.* Is Prince Marco diTalora here? It's important that I speak with him immediately."

Amanda Hutton tried to ignore the subtle—and the not-so-subtle —stares of San Rimini's high-rolling gamblers as she asked the manager of the elite Casino Campione the same question she'd discreetly posed at three other gaming halls in the last hour.

If she didn't find the wayward prince and get him to the Duomo, pronto, the wedding between the tiny country's crown prince, Antony diTalora, and her best friend, Jennifer Allen, would be delayed. Even with two hundred guests descending on the country's famed cathedral, the ceremony could hardly start without the best man in attendance.

She fought impatience as the heavyset manager studied her with irritation in his eyes. He acted no differently than the other three managers had as he took in the sight of her formal, rose-colored gown and matching shoes. Designed for a royal wedding, it wasn't an ordinary maid of honor's gown, to be sure, but neither was the cut comparable to the Valentino and Chanel couture sported by San Rimini's social elite as they made their way through the aisles of blackjack and craps tables, expensive drinks in hand.

After hearing three clipped answers of "*no*," from managers at other casinos in response to her inquiries, she wasn't about to waste time while manager number four attempted to gauge the value of her clothes and jewelry.

"Please," she began, assuming the manager spoke English in addition to San Rimini's Italian, "I realize there are privacy concerns, but I—"

"Your name?" He raised an overgrown eyebrow as if to say, *how dare you make a demand of me?*

"Amanda. Amanda Hutton. As I was about to explain, I was sent by—"

"You should know, Amanda Hutton, that when Prince Marco is a guest of this establishment, he is not to be disturbed." He punctuated his statement with a patronizing smile, as if he fielded such inquiries from women on an hourly basis, and the name Amanda Hutton did not rate.

Even so, Amanda's pulse upped a notch. Not only did this manager speak perfect English, the swagger in his voice said that he was hosting Prince Marco.

Before she could explain the delicate situation, he added, "Perhaps you could wait outside. With the others." He gestured past the ringing slot machines toward a long row of glass-and-brass revolving doors leading to San Rimini's most famous thoroughfare, the Strada il Teatro.

She followed the line of his arm. Several young women in sexy, summery dresses lingered outside. A few pulled at their hair, artfully arranging the strands over their shoulders, while others checked teeth or makeup using their phone cameras. All appeared to be waiting for a glimpse of Prince Marco. Or the chance to slip him their phone numbers.

Amanda flashed a conciliatory smile and replied, "Of course. I'm sorry to have disturbed you."

The manager nodded his acceptance, but glowered until Amanda turned and walked toward the exit.

Scouring the main room of the posh gaming hall as she went, she spied a staircase along one wall. A tall armed guard stood off to the side. He kept his thumb hooked casually in his belt loop while he spoke with a patron, but one eye remained on the steps. Amanda figured either the casino kept its cash up those stairs or that was where the private gambling rooms were located.

She hoped it was the latter.

Under the manager's watchful gaze, Amanda exited the casino, but kept close to the door, standing near the loitering women as if she stalked princes every day.

Unfortunately, the manager didn't budge from his position in the center of the casino floor, leaving her little hope of getting back indoors undetected.

Amanda strode to the curb, then shielded her eyes against the bright sunshine to read the clock on the tower adjoining La Rocca di Zaffiro, San Rimini's royal palace, which sat atop a hill less than a fifteen-minute walk to the west.

Three-thirty. With only an hour until the ceremony, there was no way she could explain the situation to the casino manager without embarrassing the royal family. Not that the manager even cared to listen.

She could kill Prince Marco. How could the manager—how could the entire country—not know where he should be at this moment? For the last eight years, since she'd graduated from college, Amanda had worked with the children of dignitaries. In all that time, she'd never come across a child as irresponsible as this prince. And he was twenty-five.

"My one vacation," she grumbled to herself. This week was her opportunity to get away from it all—to visit one of the world's most beautiful countries, participate in her best friend's wedding, and rub elbows with several of Europe's most rich and famous. But instead of spending the afternoon nibbling on canapés and having her hair done, she was running around San Rimini in an atrociously uncomfortable pair of shoes, hunting down a spoiled prince who'd gone gambling instead of attending the groom. Prince Marco hadn't appeared at his brother's lunchtime reception to welcome the VIPs who'd traveled to

San Rimini to attend the wedding, and now, even if she managed to get the prince to the Duomo in time for the ceremony itself, she'd be a sweaty mess.

Correction: a sweaty mess with blistered feet who would be expected to look perfect in the wedding pictures.

This was not the break she'd imagined before she had to return to reality and her overdue rent back in Washington, D.C.

A wave of giggles rose from the waiting women. Amanda ignored them and returned her attention to the casino's interior.

A well-dressed patron now occupied the manager. The woman waved one bracelet-laden arm to indicate an area toward the rear wall of the casino. The manager repeatedly shook his head, then held a finger aloft as he made a call on his cell phone. Annoyance narrowed his eyes, then he pocketed his phone, said something to the woman, and followed her out of view of the front entrance.

Making the most of the opportunity, Amanda pushed through the revolving door and made a beeline for the staircase.

The guard who'd been keeping an eye on the stairs snapped to attention. "May I help you?"

From his demeanor, Amanda could tell he wasn't about to let her see Prince Marco, either. She hesitated a moment, then said, "I hope so. Those women out front? They're here to see Prince Marco."

The guard's mouth crooked on one side. "What of it?"

"Well, I heard one of them say she knew which car the prince arrived in, and that the doors were left unlocked. She was going to try to sneak into the back seat and wait for him. I thought someone official should know."

The guard studied her for a moment while Amanda did her best to look like an earnest guest. However, instead of leaving to check out the women, as Amanda had hoped, he lifted a hand to the side of his head and pressed a button on an earpiece. A second later, his cell phone buzzed, and he began speaking in rapid San Riminian-accented Italian. Amanda understood just enough to realize that the guard intended to stay put.

A few words of response echoed back over the phone. The guard paused, then frowned at Amanda. "What does she look like?"

"Brunette in a green and yellow dress. Not very tall. Close to my height," she improvised, knowing none of the women out front fit that description. "I believe she went around the side of the building, maybe to check out the parking lot. She didn't say. If you need me to identify her, I'd be happy to wait here while you check."

He hesitated, and she quickly pointed down to her shoes. "I'd go along, but I don't think I'd be able to keep up with you in these heels. I can barely walk across the casino. I went out front because I'd decided to call for a ride, but heard the women talking when I was searching for the number."

Instead of answering Amanda, he repeated her description into the phone, listened for a moment, then ended the call. When she continued to stand there, he said, "It's being investigated. Thank you."

"Oh. Good. Do you want me to stay, just in case they need me to confirm the description?"

His shrug translated to a combination of *do what you want* and *the parking lot is not my job.*

At that moment, a commotion began out front. Both Amanda and the guard looked in time to see one of the women push another's shoulder. It was apparent from the body language of those around them that the women had already had words, but the situation had escalated.

Amanda indicated a red leather stool in front of an empty slot machine. "I'll wait here."

The guard didn't appear to register her statement as he strode toward the front doors, his hand going to his earpiece. It was obvious he wasn't going outside himself, only reporting what he saw so others could handle the situation. Figuring it was her only chance, Amanda waited until his back was fully turned, then bolted up the narrow staircase. The instant she reached the top, she bit back a curse. At least a dozen closed doors lined the carpeted hallway in front of her. How could she possibly guess which room held the prince?

The guard would return to his post any moment. Given the abrupt nature of her disappearance, she was sure he'd poke his head upstairs to ensure she hadn't come this way.

She made her way down the hall as quickly and quietly as possible, pausing at each doorway to listen. Several of the doors were marked with names on brass plaques designating them as offices. The others, however, were designated as suites, each named after a local celebrity. She had her ear pressed to one named after a famous oceanographer when, from the far end of the hallway, she heard the unmistakable sound of gamblers cheering a big win. After glancing behind her to make sure the guard hadn't followed, she approached the suite where she thought the sound originated. Unlike the others, this door was simply marked *Privato*.

She waited a moment, listening. At first the voices were hard to distinguish, then a woman's voice rose above the others to announce in English, "The dealer has blackjack," followed by a few grumbles. Amanda pushed on the lever handle. When it gave, she peered inside.

Sure enough, as if it had been modeled on a scene from a James Bond movie, the sumptuous, modern suite was designed to cater to gamblers whose wealth warranted a private space for gaming. To Amanda's left, a fully-stocked bar covered one wall, and a uniformed bartender stood behind its smooth black granite countertop polishing highball glasses to a spotless finish. Crystal wall sconces cast the room in a soft light, and a thick gray carpet muffled footfalls to preserve the quiet atmosphere.

Opposite her, white silk curtains framed three floor-to-ceiling windows, each of which offered a stunning view of San Rimini Bay and the Adriatic Sea beyond.

She shifted her focus to the room's interior, where no one seemed to notice her unannounced arrival. In the center stood a lone black-jack table, manned by a leggy blonde in a short black skirt, black vest, and immaculate white oxford shirt. The four seated gamblers appeared to be in their mid-twenties to early thirties, and were well-dressed in tailored tuxedos and white shirts. Amanda immediately identified Prince Marco diTalora.

He was far better-looking than the palace's official portrait portrayed him.

He sat with his jaw propped on the heel of his hand, his fingers thrust into sun-kissed blond waves of hair just above his ear. Intelligent, steel-blue eyes studied the movements of the dealer as she ran her hand across the felt table, silently requesting the men place their bets.

Prince Marco straightened, then shoved a large pile of chips forward. His mouth curved into a smile when the man next to him threw him a teasing elbow. The prince had full lips—very kissable lips, Amanda decided—and white, Hollywood-straight teeth. His tanned cheekbones were high and well-defined, like a model's, although unlike many male models, Marco was no teenage beanpole ready to strut down a runway. His broad shoulders filled his tuxedo to perfection.

She took a second look at his hair now that his hands weren't in it. Tousled a bit, as if he'd just clambered out of bed and smoothed it with his fingers, the style didn't scream wealth. The top button on his shirt was undone and his bow tie hung loose.

The powers that be at the palace either made him see a barber prior to his formal portrait sitting, or the shot was taken during his military service. Though Marco possessed a prince's self-assured bearing, she suspected he preferred the rough-and-tumble look to something more refined.

Straitlaced as Amanda was, she decided she preferred it on him, too. The hair reflected his easygoing body language. Even so, he needed to look regal, and fast, to keep the ceremony from being delayed. She took a deep, centering breath, then eased all the way into the room.

"*Mi scusi*, Prince Marco," she began. "I was—"

"Leaving." Amanda jumped as the guard, face flushed with anger, curled his fingers around her arm, just above the elbow. "*Mi dispiace*, Your Highness. I allowed myself to be distracted, and she ran up from the main floor. It will not happen again." The guard gave Amanda a withering look, then began to pull her into the hall.

"Please," Amanda called over her shoulder to the prince as she braced a hand against the door frame. "I was sent—"

"*Va bene*, Ivan. Let her stay."

Marco surprised her by flicking a quick look at the guard, who immediately released his death grip on her arm.

"But...yes, of course, Prince Marco." The confused guard bowed, then spun on his heel, presumably to return to his post.

The prince turned to the table, attention riveted on the game as the dealer dealt him a king.

Amanda peeled her fingers from the door frame, then slowly moved toward the table. The men were intent on the game, but she couldn't wait any longer. "Your Highness, as I was saying, I was sent by—"

"You must be Ms. Hutton." The prince didn't look away from the cards. "I'm sorry, I don't remember your first name. I haven't forgotten the wedding. I'll be done in a minute. Feel free to order a drink." He absently waved her toward the bar.

Amanda did a double take. His English was amazing—he sounded as American as she did—and apparently he knew her name—sort of—and had expected her arrival.

"How'd you know I'd be here?"

He laughed, though his eyes didn't leave the cards in front of him. "Antony's wedding can't be more than a couple hours off. I figured either he or Jennifer would send someone once I missed lunch."

"Wish I'd skipped that lunch myself," one of the men commented. "One of the columnists from *Today's Royals* cornered me for nearly fifteen minutes. What's her name...Val Dempsey? Getting into a conversation with her is like being handcuffed to a wall. There's no escape. And do you know who else was there?" He named a French actress, then bemoaned the fact that she hadn't been the one to corner him. Or handcuff him.

While another of the men added his thoughts on the French actress and handcuffs, Marco gave Amanda a quick up and down. "I assume you're the maid of honor. My brother told me repeatedly that the maid of honor was American. Jennifer's college roommate. And her name was" —he snapped his fingers— "*Amanda* Hutton."

Amanda wavered, unsure of her next move. She'd only thought about locating the missing prince, not about what she'd actually say when she found him. She needed to convince him to leave now, not a drink or two from now.

"Actually, Prince Marco," she tried to explain, "we only have an hour. Probably less now that—"

The dealer flipped over a second king for Marco.

Amanda took an involuntary step back as Marco's gambling buddies let out a raucous cheer. She'd only played blackjack once before, on a weekend trip to Atlantic City after college, but knew a good hand when she saw one. Since the dealer showed a seven up, and the best she'd likely do was seventeen, he'd scored a big victory.

Mentally tallying the number of black chips in the pile he'd shoved forward, she figured he'd gambled about six months' worth of her earnings. Before taxes.

Marco ignored the cheers. Instead, he counted out another massive stack of chips and set it next to the first.

"Split them."

"*Folle!*" The man who'd complained about the columnist shook his head, and even though Amanda's Italian was limited, she knew enough to agree with the assessment. His decision was folly. Madness.

The second man said, "You want to throw away your money, Marco, I can think of better ways."

The dealer's eyebrows moved fractionally higher, but she said nothing. She separated the two kings so they lay side by side, then pulled a card from the shoe and laid it on the first king.

"A six for sixteen."

She drew another card, placing it on the second king. "And sixteen again."

Marco's friends groaned in unison.

The final gambler spoke up, his English tinged with a British accent. "Sorry, Marco. Good thing you can afford it, mate."

The dealer finished with the other players, then turned over her own card.

"Seven and four for eleven—"

"You'd better not get twenty-one twice in a row," the British man interrupted. "I might not be able to explain to my wife why we can't afford a proper gift for the royal couple."

The dealer smiled, but continued to flip cards. "And two for thirteen, and a queen for twenty-three. Bust."

A whoop went up around the table.

"Now my wife will like that," the British man said, clapping the prince on the shoulder. "What possessed you?"

Marco gave a nonchalant shrug. "It was my last hand. Thought I'd make a go of it."

He pulled back his shirt sleeve to reveal a thick tan line where his watch should be. "Well, no wonder I'm running late. Must've left it at home. You gentlemen better hurry if you want to get seated." He tipped the dealer a few black chips just as the casino manager entered the room. The portly man glared at Amanda for a split second, then bowed to Marco, all smiles. "Has everything been satisfactory, Your Highness?"

"Rafaella did her job extraordinarily well, as always. Perhaps she should get a raise." The flirtatious wink he threw to the dealer made Amanda want to gag.

"Of course, of course," the manager nodded, only too anxious to please the prince. "Shall I cash in your chips, or would you prefer to have the amount deposited in your account?"

"The account," he replied, easing off the stool with more grace than Amanda thought possible for a gambling, never-one-to-miss-a-good-party twenty-something. Perhaps he had learned a few social niceties being a prince.

Or, at least, whichever social skills best helped him attract women. The dealer's eyes were firmly on the prince's rear as he turned his back to the table.

The manager began gathering the prince's chips, but Marco clapped the man on the shoulder before he could finish. "I've changed my mind. Please see that the money is sent to the San Riminian Scholarship Fund at Banca Nazionale. Make it an anonymous donation in honor of Prince Antony's wedding to Jennifer Allen. And you" —he held up a warning finger and looked at his companions one by one, before his gaze settled on Amanda— "don't breathe a word. I mean it when I say this is anonymous."

The men murmured their agreement. Amanda did the same, though Jennifer would be curious about the source of the large donation to the charity she and Prince Antony supported. Knowing Jennifer, she'd investigate until she learned the mysterious donor's identity. But given the impression Amanda had of the prince so far, it could take a while. She couldn't imagine Jennifer suspecting Marco of making the contribution.

"I would be honored to take care of it in person, Your Highness," the casino manager said, bowing lower than necessary.

"Thank you, but I would rather you send someone. And do not mention that the deposit is from the Casino Campione."

The manager's smile slipped a notch as he straightened, but he maintained his composure. "As you wish."

"Well then, I have a wedding to attend." He buttoned the top of his shirt, tied his bow tie—without need of a mirror, Amanda noted— then gestured for her to walk ahead of him to the door. "Ms. Hutton?"

As they entered the hall, he pulled the front of his tuxedo jacket taut, sending the faintest whiff of cologne her way. Whatever he wore was both enticing and surprisingly understated.

"That was generous of you."

"Guilty is more like it," he confessed. "I've been snorkeling in Greece for the last week. Didn't have time to get a proper gift. Just some silly crystal candlesticks my father suggested."

Amanda forced herself not to point out the obvious: that he'd had time to gamble. Still, the gift was generous. Knowing Antony and Jennifer, they'd appreciate it far more than the candlesticks.

Marco ran a hand through his hair, unfortunately leaving it more ruffled than before. "Do I look ready for a royal wedding?"

"I'm sure you'll do, Your Highness." Amanda tried not to gawk at him. She was used to dealing with the social elite in her job. She'd even spent a month at the White House teaching the president's children how to handle themselves with foreign dignitaries. As the daughter of a former ambassador herself, she'd grown up surrounded by those in power.

Still, nothing had prepared her for Prince Marco. He was about as unroyal as a royal could be. If she'd simply run into him at the wedding, without seeing his picture beforehand, she'd have mistaken him for a good-looking party crasher instead of a member of San Rimini's royal family. The type of party crasher who usually disappeared with a bridesmaid at the end of the evening.

"I'll do? Haven't heard that one before. You're supposed to tell me I look fabulous. Sexy." He shot her a confident grin. "At least say, 'Of course, Your Highness,' or 'Nice tux, Your Highness.' Not just that I'll do."

She hazarded a glance at him. He towered nearly a foot over her, at around six-foot-two. Maybe even six-three. With his disheveled hair, gigantic bank account, and impeccable bloodlines, she was certain women did find him sexy. *She* thought he was sexy, despite his behavior. But she wasn't about to tell him so, not in the tight confines of a narrow casino hallway.

And certainly not when he seemed well aware of his own attractiveness.

"Where did you learn your English?" she asked instead. "You sound as if you could've grown up next door to Wally and the Beav. I've met your brothers, and they both speak more formally. And with accents."

His raised brow indicated he was well aware of her attempt to change the subject. "Antony and Federico picked up their early English from their nanny, who was from London, and were educated here and in Italy, where the majority of their professors spoke British English. I had an American nanny, then went to school in the States, though I didn't see a single rerun of 'Leave It to Beaver.' Is it even on television anymore?"

Amanda was surprised he got the reference. Most of her friends

out on the seat between them. Then, leaning across her, he gathered another bunch of material and dropped it to fall in a wave between her side of the seat and the passenger door.

"See?" he raised his hands again, hoping she'd realize his intentions were innocent. "No sense in letting the maid of honor get wrinkled before the main event."

"No, I suppose not." She offered him a half smile, but it disappeared as he took her fisted hands and gently raised them off her lap.

"Let it go," he instructed. She blinked, then after a split second of hesitation, did as he asked and released the fabric she'd been clutching.

He flashed her what he hoped was an I'm-no-threat-to-you smile, then leaned forward to capture the area near the hem and gave the front of the dress a quick shake.

"Voilà," he waved his hand over her lap as if he'd completed a magic trick. "Even the palace buzzards can't criticize you now. You'll look fabulous in all the photos."

She looked down at her dress, then back at him as the Range Rover turned off the Strada il Teatro onto a bumpy cobblestone street. "Thank you."

"You're welcome. The least I could do, given that any wrinkles would be my fault." He gave her a sideways look. She still seemed skittish. "That being said, if I touch you again, please don't assume the worst of me. We'll be expected to dance together at the reception. I don't know what the security staff would do if you started screaming."

"I promise, no screaming." This time, her smile was genuine, reaching all the way to her eyes. "But if you get out of line, all bets are off."

He had to grin. Even with her uptight attitude, he'd immediately sensed she had a backbone. Backbone enough to sneak past Ivan and enter the private gaming room. Enough to make that crack about UNLV. And now, enough to threaten him if he touched her in a way that even hinted at seduction.

"Fine," he replied. "But remember when you say, 'All bets are off,' that I'm the gambler, not you."

That did it. She finally relaxed enough to laugh aloud, and he liked the musical sound of it.

He studied her for a moment. The name Amanda suited her. A romantic name for a woman who looked as if she'd been born to play the lead in a boy-meets-girl movie, with her perfect posture, full lips and soft brown hair that begged to be mussed.

But the oddest part of it was that he found himself more intrigued by her willingness to speak her mind than by her physical attributes.

He met gorgeous women every day. Due to his position, he had the chance to be with any of them he chose. They practically leapt in his lap, showering him with superficial praise now that he was done with his army stint and had returned home to San Rimini. But how many years had it been since anyone, male or female, had the guts to speak to him as if he were their friend or coworker instead of a prince?

Besides his primary school buddies—now his gambling and skiing buddies—who'd gotten to know him when his mother was alive and had enrolled him in public school, he couldn't think of a soul.

Amanda's gaze locked with his, and he felt a sudden, over-whelming urge to touch her leg once more. And this time, not just to adjust her gown.

The apples of her cheeks slowly blushed crimson, and he realized he sat mostly on her side of the back seat. Way too close for her comfort, or his own.

If she could read his thoughts…well, he wouldn't have to wait for their dance to see if she'd scream in terror.

He edged to his side of the car, then glanced out the window. "We'll be there in a couple minutes. If anyone can get us to the Duomo on time, it's Filippo. He knows all the shortcuts."

They turned onto a narrower cobblestone street that cut through San Rimini's market district, bringing them toward the rear of the stunning cathedral. Shopkeepers on the tiny streets hurried customers out of their stores, pulling the metal gates down behind the stragglers so they could get home in time to see the wedding on television. A group of tourists waved San Riminian flags as they strolled downhill toward the Strada il Teatro, where the royal couple would take a carriage ride following the ceremony.

"I suppose he has to use these shortcuts quite frequently," Amanda commented as they took a sharp curve. She shot him a questioning look and grabbed her door's armrest as Filippo braked for a pack of jaywalkers.

"My apologies," he said.

"No, we're the ones who should apologize," Amanda told Filippo, her voice sincere. "I appreciate that you're driving us in such crowded conditions. Thank you."

"You're welcome," he replied, tipping a nod to her in the mirror.

His voice low, Marco asked, "Are you insinuating that I frequently run late?"

"I said no such thing."

"Doesn't matter. We're here." Marco nodded toward the front of the car as the Range Rover slowed to a stop outside a police barricade. Filippo rolled down his window, motioning for the officer to let them pass. Marco leaned forward, gauging the security presence before eyeing the clock on the dash. "And with nearly twenty minutes to spare."

"That's *all?*" she gasped. "Jennifer must be incredibly worried. And I won't have any time to freshen up."

Filippo waved his thanks as the officer allowed the Range Rover through the barricade and into an alley that ended at the Duomo's small parking area, which was only used for staff and dignitaries at special events. "Do it now. You've got a minute."

She frowned, eyed her purse, then shook her head. "Thanks, but it's really not proper. I'd feel more comfortable waiting until we get inside."

"It's not *proper?* Who cares?"

"I do."

He frowned. "Why? Because you're sitting next to a prince?"

"Because it's my job."

"Freshening up?"

"No, of course not. I'm a children's etiquette expert, if you must know. I try to live what I teach."

No wonder she never seemed to unwind. And no wonder she didn't seem to find him attractive. She probably thought he was a complete boor. "You're one of those, are you? Like the palace buzzards? I should have known you'd be the type to lecture kids about which fork they should use for salad and which for dessert."

"I never lecture," she said, craning her neck to take in the rear of the Duomo as she spoke. From here, they were buffered from the crowds that had gathered outside the front steps in hopes of seeing the bride and groom exit following the ceremony, but the noise still carried, even though the car windows. Amanda straightened, then shrugged. "What I do goes far beyond forks, I assure you. I help children of dignitaries—ambassadors, congressmen, the judiciary—deal with the day-to-day problems of being born to someone in the public eye."

"Such as their swelled heads? That must be challenging."

She looked him up and down, her thoughts on that subject all too apparent.

He'd walked right into that one. "Touché, Ms. Hutton."

She shook her head, and a cinnamon-colored curl bounced loose over her ear as she did so. "Well, present company excluded, of course—"

"Of course."

"But you're right. Some of them do have swelled heads," she admitted. "I give them aspirin for that."

He stared at her, caught off guard by the joke.

She quickly waved it off, as if fearing it had fallen flat. "That's an issue I leave for the parents. My focus is on helping my clients better navigate social interactions. While I'm certainly capable of explaining behavioral norms that help them avoid embarrassment—you know, the which-fork-do-I-use? predicament—and I will answer those questions if they need help, they've usually already mastered those lessons by the time I'm called. What I do is more subtle."

"How so?"

A slight smile lifted the corners of her mouth. "I teach them how to converse comfortably at public events. I also help them identify people who are after their family's money or connections, or who might be fishing for personal information, that kind of thing."

"I see." He knew the type all too well. Even well-respected members of San Rimini's upper class had approached him at royal functions when he was a teenager, trying to attach themselves to him for the express purpose of gaining access to his parents or picking up inside information. More than once, he'd fallen into their traps, telling them things he probably shouldn't have.

"And once your faithful students learn to identify these leeches?" he asked. "Then what?"

"Mostly we run through scenarios they're likely to encounter so they have tools to handle different situations. Ever so politely, of course. There's an art to dissuading people who want to use you while maintaining a friendly attitude. The children I work with can't offend those who might be important to their parents' careers, but they need to protect themselves." She shrugged. "It's a difficult skill for a parent to teach a child, which is where I come in. It's a tightrope walk that can be uncomfortable at times, and it takes practice, you know?"

"All too well," he murmured.

How many times had he avoided palace soirées—state dinners, charity events, debutante balls—and opted to go skiing or boating with his friends, hoping to avoid playing politics or inadvertently offending someone who might be important to his father's goals? The whole idea put him in a cold sweat. His mother had always handled such situations with aplomb, particularly for someone not born into a royal family, but to her credit, she'd recognized that Marco didn't and let him skip all but the essential engagements. He wished she could be here to advise him now. The conclusion of his military duties meant he'd be expected to take on political ones. Soon.

When Amanda spoke again, her voice was soft. "You were away at university when your mother passed away, weren't you?"

Was the woman a mind reader as well? He met her gaze, and instantly realized it didn't take a mind reader to know what bothered him. It simply took a woman who possessed his mother's skill for reading the emotions of those around her. He'd been wearing his heart on his sleeve.

"I'd just started at Princeton when she was diagnosed. I went in with a number of credits and took a heavy load my first semester, so I was able to take off the spring semester and spend it in San Rimini, which was when her health took a nosedive. Isabella was in her final year of university in London, and my mother insisted she stay and graduate with her class. Federico and Lucrezia were newlyweds and had traveled to Australia and New Zealand on their first state visit as a married couple. Antony was in Africa on a diplomatic mission. They've never said so, but I'm sure being away made it harder on them."

She shifted in her seat. "Still, alone at home with a grieving father and the press crawling all over the country. It must have been difficult."

"Probably would've helped to have had your services, even if they are meant for children. But I managed. We all did." He cleared his throat, unwilling to look at her any longer. There was too much temptation there. Temptation to take a second look, or a third, at someone who was not only beautiful, but possessed his mother's best qualities. For reasons that were deeply personal, he'd sworn to himself long ago that he'd never date a woman like that. He intended to keep that promise.

Better to stick with the cute-but-vapid women who mooned over him. If, at some point, his father insisted he marry...well, he'd cross that bridge when he came to it. Fortunately, with Antony's wedding today, and the fact Federico was not only married, but a father of two, the odds of that happening had dropped.

The Range Rover pulled to a stop, and Marco gestured toward the side door, where guards screened invited guests. "Anyway, why don't you put on your lipstick or whatever it is you women do to freshen up, if you feel the need. I won't tell anyone." He winked and added, "Besides, with the jet set attending this party, you're sure to find a new client or two. They'll be far better students than I ever would have been."

———

Marco had been right about one thing, Amanda noted as she laid her sterling silver fork across her dessert plate, indicating that the waiter could take it away. More potential clients were in attendance than she'd imagined, given the wedding's relatively small guest list of two hundred. She needed to find a discreet way to mention her services before everyone went home, and hope for interest. Otherwise, she'd need to seriously consider moving back home with her parents. While her occupation paid well when she had a client, those clients could be few and far between, and she'd burned through a chunk of her savings during the last dry spell. She didn't want to see another chunk disappear.

Shaking the depressing thought from her head, she took a sip of her champagne and scanned the palace garden. Jennifer and Antony had opted to host their reception here, rather than in the more formal Imperial Ballroom. Other than Jennifer's parents, who'd spent their careers with charitable organizations, and a group of former refugees who'd lived at the camp where Jennifer had served as director, the majority of the guests were European aristocracy. Amanda recognized King Carlo and Queen Fabrizia of Sarcaccia, two members of the Dutch royal family, and San Rimini's Ambassador to the United States.

Members of the Royal Orchestra played on the stairs leading from the palace into the garden, filling the evening air with graceful music. The groom, Prince Antony, was having his picture taken with his brother Federico's two sons, while his father, King Eduardo, chatted with members of San Rimini's parliament.

"Man, did I ever need this break. Good thinking on your part, telling those women I deserved a slice of my own wedding cake," Jennifer leaned over and whispered, her elegant wedding gown rustling as she tried to inconspicuously rub her feet under the table. It was the first time either of them had taken a seat in hours.

"I suspected you were getting tired," Amanda said, smiling at her friend. "I figured it was my job to give you a brief respite."

"Not tired, really," Jennifer said on a sigh. "Overwhelmed. If I dance with one more famous person, I'll die. I don't care if I'm a member of the royal family now. All this celebrity will take a bit of getting used to."

At that moment, Princess Isabella and two of her friends walked by their table, each wearing a small fortune in diamond jewelry.

"They're still getting used to me, too," Jennifer added once Antony's younger sister was out of earshot. "It's not every day a gawky American comes parading into their society and marries the crown prince."

Amanda took a second look at Prince Antony, who kept glancing at their table, unable to take his eyes off his new wife. The wedding had gone off without a hitch, with a seamless transition to the reception. Young couples crowded the area of the lawn set aside for dancing, the older guests enjoyed the chance for conversation, and Jennifer had to be the most lovely, poised bride Amanda had ever seen. "If you want my expert opinion…?"

"Always."

"You'll do beautifully. Prince Antony loves you, anyone can see that. And his family loves you, too."

Jennifer reached over and squeezed Amanda's hand. "I know. They've been wonderful to me." She blinked a few times to clear her eyes of tears, then let go of Amanda's hand. They watched the garden in silence for a moment before Jennifer said, "Speaking of Antony's family, thank you for tracking down Marco. You saved the day."

"No problem." At least not a problem she'd discuss with the bride on her wedding day, no matter how close their friendship.

"You two cut it awfully close. Antony was going nuts. Then again, I told him he should have expected it. That's Marco."

Amanda hesitated, unwilling to say anything that might be interpreted as derogatory about a member of Jennifer's new family. "Well," feel you need to stay here because Jennifer left. I think there are others who would like your attention."

Marco stole a look at the parliament member and Eliza Schipani, then said, "I'm sure it's nothing urgent. Besides, I was planning to take a walk. Stretch my legs, get some fresh air. Would you care to join me?"

Alone with the sexy prince? Enticing. But not smart.

"We're in a garden. There isn't enough fresh air here?"

He lifted a brow, as if in a dare. "The gardens extend beyond the area being used for the reception. There are quieter sections. Probably several you haven't seen."

She forced herself not to look away. His eyes shone an intense blue under the lights that had been strung around the lawn for the reception. "That's true," she admitted. "And I appreciate the invitation, but I should probably stay here and wait for Jennifer. It's getting late, and she might need me."

Amanda thought she saw a look of desperation pass over his face, but it disappeared so quickly she questioned whether it was a trick of the light. Could he really experience the same discomfort in high-pressure social situations as some of her teenaged clients? She'd suspected it for a moment in the car, but had dismissed the idea. Then again, it could explain why he seemed ill at ease with the curvy blonde…who was stunning and made no secret of her interest in him, but who also happened to be considering a run for parliament.

Amanda's curiosity was piqued.

"Tell you what, why don't we make it a short walk? Just so I'm back before Jennifer is done speaking with your father." That should give her time to do some subtle networking.

Marco flashed her a heart-stopping smile. "Wonderful."

MARCO INHALED a deep lungful of the sweet night air as he led Amanda under one of the archways that marked the entrance to the rose garden. As a child, he'd been obsessed with the smell of this section. Light perfume from the rose blossoms combined with the tang of the clipped boxwood lining the gravel pathways to relax him. On nights such as this, where a warm breeze came off San Rimini Bay, he strongly preferred the garden to the suffocating air of the palace rooms, most of which were filled with statues, vases, and Renaissance-era paintings of his long-dead ancestors.

He'd never have admitted his love of the garden to his family, though. His sister Isabella, who spent much of her time here, would tease him incessantly if she knew he could identify nearly all of the garden's four hundred rose varieties without peeking at the markers.

"Wow," Amanda murmured beside him. "Seeing the garden up close is an entirely different experience than looking at it on the Internet or a postcard. The roses all look so perfect. I'm surprised there are so many blooms this late in the season. But I guess your weather's warmer than ours." She leaned over to sniff a large white hybrid tea rose, then pointed to the ground. "Who thought to put these little lights under all the plants?"

"My mother," Marco replied, "though it was Isabella who arranged to have them installed. Mother thought it would make the garden more attractive at night for parties, as well as making it more..." He managed to clamp his mouth shut before the word *romantic* popped out. His parents may have once courted here, taking long walks along the winding paths, but the last thing he wanted with Amanda Hutton was romance. Besides, he reminded himself, he'd only asked her out here to escape Eliza and her parliamentary cohorts.

If the gregarious blonde had seen him leave the reception by himself, he was certain she'd have followed him in her never-ending efforts to rope him into speaking at her next health conference. Not exactly his idea of a good time.

"Making it more...?" Amanda prompted.

"More...oh, more safe," he hastily finished, then gave her a side-long wink. "You know, muggers and such."

"Muggers?" She laughed aloud, and once again he found the sound entrancing. "This place is surrounded by a twelve-foot wrought-iron fence topped with I-don't-know-how-many cameras. And there must

CHAPTER 4

AMANDA'S BREATH felt heavy in her lungs as King Eduardo opened the French doors to his study and gestured for her to take a seat. He hadn't uttered a word as they'd made their way from the garden into the palace, then down three different hallways and past two guards before entering his private wing. Once there, he'd used a keypad to enter what turned out to be his residence.

As she took her seat, she knew this wasn't just his study, where he was often photographed with dignitaries. It was his private study. Part of his inner sanctum.

What have I gotten myself into? He wouldn't have called her here by herself if it wasn't important. Was it because she and Marco had been so late to the wedding? She was dying to ask, but etiquette dictated the king speak first.

A tall man with thick, dark hair that was going to salt and pepper, King Eduardo made an intimidating figure in the custom-made tuxedo and royal sash he wore for his eldest son's wedding. But even if he'd been strolling along a beach wearing shorts and a T-shirt, Amanda was certain no one could mistake him for anything but what he was: a man who controlled everything, and everyone, around him.

She studied his features as she lowered herself into one of the chairs, which was covered in a soft beige velvet. As with most who held positions of power, the king's outward expression revealed little of his inner thoughts.

The king didn't take the chair opposite hers, as she'd expected. Instead, he paced along one wall of the study, which was covered floor-to-ceiling in leather-bound books.

It had to be her tardy arrival to the wedding. What else could it possibly be? The king hadn't seen Prince Marco kiss her hand. She'd heard his footsteps as he'd approached along the gravel path and knew he hadn't had the proper vantage point to see them under the rose-covered arch.

She blinked, envisioning Marco's lips pressed to the inside of her wrist, remembering the feel of his solid, strong chest beneath her palm.

The sensation had rocked her to her core, but she could smack herself for allowing it to happen. Prince Marco diTalora was reckless. Five years her junior. And she'd been seconds away from tumbling right into his arms.

If the king had seen them, she'd be in even tougher straits than she was now. She knew from Jennifer's experience that he wasn't thrilled to see his children engage in public displays of affection, given that anyone with a camera could capture a shot for the tabloids.

Amanda waited until the king stopped pacing to stand behind his desk. For a moment, the only sound in the room was the distant music that emanated from the garden reception.

He fingered a photograph of his late wife, Queen Aletta. Without looking at Amanda, he asked, "I haven't seen your parents in many years, Ms. Hutton. I hope they are well?"

"They are." Her answer didn't hide her surprise at the question. "I didn't know you were acquainted."

The king nodded, though his mind seemed elsewhere. "Your father was ambassador to Italy when I ascended the throne. He and your mother attended my coronation. You were a young girl then. I believe you stayed behind in Rome."

"Of course. How kind of you to remember." She'd forgotten the event herself. It had seemed insignificant at the time, given what was happening in her life.

He continued to toy with the gilt-framed photo. "Your family left Italy soon afterward, as I recall. I'd invited your parents to return to the palace, but they were unable to come."

"My mother and her sister were diagnosed with breast cancer within a month of each other. My father felt it best to leave his position in Italy and return to the U.S., given the circumstances."

"Understandable." The king raised his head to study her. "But both women are well now?"

"Yes, thank you." Though they were vigilant about detecting a recurrence, both women were alive and well. And so was Amanda herself, despite the fact she'd been tested and found to carry the same mutated gene as her mother and aunt, a gene that indicated she was predisposed to the disease. Fortunately, science offered her an advantage they didn't have: advance knowledge.

"Ah. Good." The king's forehead creased in concentration. "I'm curious. *Parla l'italiano?*"

She shook her head. "Very little. I'd only attended my Italian school a few months when we returned to Washington."

"I see."

He hesitated for a moment, then picked up Queen Aletta's picture and turned it on the desk for her to see. "This picture was taken of Marco's mother on our wedding day. I loved her with all my heart. Unfortunately, she died of ovarian cancer nearly six years ago, as I'm sure you recall."

The press had covered the beautiful queen's death with as much ink as they had Princess Grace's and Princess Diana's. "Of course, Your Highness. It was a tragedy."

"I mourned her for a long time. I think of her each day, still." He returned the photo to its place on his desk, then walked around to where she sat, finally taking the chair opposite hers. "Unfortunately, I made some mistakes after she passed away, and it is my hope you can help me rectify them."

Amanda hesitated. She hardly knew the king, yet there was a tone in his voice that said he was about to impart deeply personal information. She wasn't sure how she felt about that.

"I know you went to find Prince Marco today when he failed to appear on time for the ceremony."

"Yes."

"Do not look so worried. My children worked hard to conceal their brother's absence from me this afternoon, and I will not tell them I know of their deception." The corner of the king's mouth quirked. "Since they were young, Antony, Federico, and Isabella have hidden Marco's behavioral faults from me. Tried to keep him out of trouble when he played pranks, covered for him when he disappeared from the palace grounds or skipped official functions. They still feel the need to protect him, I suppose."

He waved a hand as he spoke, and Amanda couldn't help but notice he still wore his wedding band in addition to a large gold ring bearing the crest of the diTalora family. He might be the ruler of one of Europe's wealthiest countries, but she sensed that family was equally important to King Eduardo.

"I appreciate that you went to find him, but his outing today convinced me that something must be done." The king sat back and folded his hands in his lap. "It is my own fault. I have allowed Marco to have his head, to live with more freedom than the others."

He paused, as if unsure how much to reveal. Amanda remained silent. Finally, he said, "I was more concerned with my pain than with Marco's following Queen Aletta's death. Marco was young and, on the outside at least, seemed to recover from the shock more quickly than I. As time passed, I turned my focus to matters of state. Isabella stepped into Queen Aletta's role as palace hostess, and—prior to my heart surgery—to finding a proper bride for Antony, since he is my heir."

Amanda smiled at the king, though she was still unsure why he was telling her all this. "Prince Antony and Jennifer will be very happy together."

The king met her gaze, and the tiny lines around his eyes crinkled. "Yes, they will. That is one instance where my intrusion did not help. I allowed myself to be driven by my own fears, given that I've learned hard lessons about the transitory nature of our time here on Earth." His face grew serious again. "However, with Marco, I am afraid it's time I got involved."

The king stood, but motioned to indicate that Amanda should remain seated. He ran his fingers through his hair, and regret mingled with exasperation in his voice as he explained, "You see, I believed Prince Marco would grow more responsible with age. I assumed Princeton would mature him, but if anything, he only became more adventurous as he absorbed American culture. And his time in the San Riminian army did nothing to hone his sense of royal responsibility. Since returning home from military service, he has spent his time skiing, boating, gambling, and doing who knows what else with his friends. He has avoided all but the most essential official functions."

Amanda's gaze went to the wall of books behind the king. One shelf held a painting of the royal family as they had been roughly fifteen years before, when Marco was ten or eleven years old. The young prince stood behind his mother, his hand on her shoulder. As Amanda studied the portrait, understanding dawned.

"Perhaps," she spoke slowly, not wanting to contradict the king, "he's not as irresponsible as you believe. Perhaps he simply isn't comfortable in the palace, with what's expected of him here. When he's with his friends, he finds he can be himself."

He'd certainly seemed more at ease at the casino than here at the palace. He'd laughed and joked with his friends then, but once they'd arrived at the royal wedding, and he'd been surrounded by the aristocratic guests and members of the media, he'd quieted. Made an effort to keep himself separate from others. And then there was his invitation to walk in the rose garden.

He'd wanted to escape the endless small talk.

The king raised a dark eyebrow. "That is quite perceptive of you, Ms. Hutton, for I have also come to that conclusion."

He hesitated for a moment, then moved to stand behind the seat he'd previously occupied, bracing his hands on the back as he spoke. "In many ways, Marco has grown into a strong young man. He has firm opinions, but he listens and considers the feelings of others. And though he can be quite outgoing at times, he is careful not to show his inner thoughts. Those are all fine qualities in a prince." A tired sigh escaped the king's lips. "However, because Marco is so strong, he gives the impression that he does not need anyone. I now realize that he does, just as he needed his mother while he was young. Aletta made him comfortable in the palace, and guided him through the intricacies of living a very public life."

His gaze fixed on Amanda, and her stomach knotted as it finally dawned on her why he'd asked to see her in private.

"That is why he needs you, Ms. Hutton, though he is too stubborn and proud a man ever to admit it. You are an expert in these affairs. I want you to be his guide and show him how to be comfortable in the position he was born to occupy. Help him find his public role as a member of the royal family."

She hesitated, needing a moment to stifle her urge to gape. "You're asking me to teach your son? Prince Marco?"

"Would you consider the position?"

"Your Highness, I'm flattered, truly. But I don't work with adults." Certainly not grown men who had the power to make her pulse race merely by looking at her.

She straightened in her chair, hoping to project a tranquility she didn't feel. "I'm not sure what Jennifer has told you about my work, but my experience is with children and teenagers. It's an entirely different skill set. What you are seeking is beyond my professional purview."

Clearly used to getting his own way, the king continued as if she'd made no protest. "Your father is an honorable man, able to keep a confidence. You've shown through your career that you keep confidences, as well. You also have a personal connection to my family, which makes you the perfect candidate." He strode to the back of his desk and opened a drawer. "You know, I spoke with my new daughter-in-law while Marco showed you the rose garden. She indicated that you have excellent references and answered in the affirmative when I asked whether you were looking for new clients."

She'd kill Jennifer when she got out of the king's presence, best friend or not. Then again, the king hadn't said that he told Jennifer he was asking for Marco. Jennifer likely assumed he had a friend with young children in need of her services.

"That is true, Your Highness, however—"

"If you'll forgive me, I did some investigating prior to speaking with Jennifer. Your last professional engagement ended nearly four months ago. Rent is high in Washington, D.C., even for a modest residence. Nor are groceries, transportation, or other basics inexpensive. And then there is student loan debt, for those who have it. Four months without employment is a long time." He looked at her, then nodded to himself, as if confirming his research by her failure to deny his statement.

"Therefore," —he withdrew a piece of paper from the drawer and held it aloft— "I'm willing to offer you a substantial salary, with a contract for three months' guaranteed wages. I am willing to pay each month's salary in advance, if that is helpful to you. You will have medical care. Dental care. Full access to the palace, including the gym, hairdresser, tailor—whatever services you wish. After that period, if Marco is doing well, I shall personally ensure you find employment with a well-respected family, either here in Europe or in the United States. Your choice. If I feel Marco still needs you, we can discuss terms that will permit you to stay here as long as it takes to get the job done."

She tried not to look as stunned as she felt. He made it sound like a dream job, with the exception of the student. "Your Highness, it's truly an offer I—"

"An offer you cannot refuse, I hope. No matter that your expertise is with children. My son may be a prince, and a grown man, but he will treat you with the respect you deserve and follow your instruction. There will be no rebelliousness with this particular student."

He pushed the paper across his desk. "Will you sign the agreement?"

Amanda forced herself not to fidget as she pondered her options. How could she possibly take the job?

She wasn't worried about Marco's rebelliousness, as the king seemed to believe. It was her attraction to the prince that concerned her.

Every woman in attendance at tonight's wedding was aware of Marco's sex appeal. When she'd walked through the garden with him, Amanda had sensed that his emotions ran deep and he wasn't the shallow person others believed him to be. His good looks combined with his complex psyche to form one alluring package.

But she had to fight that allure, and fight it hard. Falling for Marco would only demonstrate her own irresponsibility, causing her to lose the job before she could even get started. If she accepted and then lost this job, she'd have an impossible time landing another.

"Your Highness, I'm not sure..." she started, but as she spoke, she met the king's eyes and realized that refusing the job might be worse.

She took a deep breath, then became conscious of the fact that she could no longer hear the orchestra playing on the stairs to the garden. The guests were leaving, meaning that tomorrow she'd return to the United States with no prospects. Another month of unemployment and she'd have to move in with her parents.

She rose from her chair and crossed to the desk.

"Do you have a pen?"

The king produced a thick ballpoint as she skimmed the contract. Everything he'd promised—an eye-popping salary, unbelievable perks —stared back at her in black and white.

"I only have one note," she said as she continued to read. "Though you are paying my salary, my policy has always been to put the children I'm tutoring first. It's my duty to teach them to be comfortable in their public role. Not to teach them how to make their parents happy with them. I consider the child—in this case, Prince Marco—to be the client. I would be teaching him to fulfill his role to the best of his ability. Not the best of your ability."

The king considered her for a long moment. Then he nodded.

Before she could second guess herself, she signed the contract.

The king added his signature to hers, then told her he'd provide her with a copy. "I will make this worth your while, Ms. Hutton. You will not regret it."

Amanda hoped the king wouldn't regret it. And who knew what Marco would think when he found out.

———

MARCO ROLLED OVER, reaching for the nightstand in a blind effort to find his phone and silence the alarm.

He swore under his breath as something sharp lanced his palm. Squinting in the morning's dim light, he saw the yellow rose and remembered.

What had possessed him to bring the thorny thing inside? He'd offered it to her, for *her* nightstand.

And he shouldn't even have done that.

He shoved aside the thick covers as he sat up, then realized that the incessant clamor wasn't his alarm, but the door buzzer to his private palace apartment. At the exact moment he made the connection, the relentless knock of a fist began. It wasn't a happy noise.

Probably Isabella, up with the birds as usual and coming to chew him out for disappearing from the reception instead of discussing politics with her friend, Eliza Schipani.

He swore under his breath. Knowing Isabella, she wouldn't leave until she'd said what she came to say. Perhaps if he apologized first thing, then promised to call Eliza if Isabella really pushed, she might cut her overbearing older sister lecture to a tolerable length.

He smoothed his hair with his hands and yawned. He should've known this would happen. If he'd been smart, he'd have arranged to drive to Austria with his friends immediately after the reception, rather than waiting for tonight.

Yanking on his robe over his boxer shorts, he made his way out of the bedroom, through his sitting room to the front door of his apartment. When he opened it, he was stunned to see his father, not Isabella, standing in the hallway.

Marco blinked. Something had to be wrong. Usually, the king

summoned his children if he needed to speak to them. He certainly didn't awaken them at the crack of dawn by ringing their buzzers and pounding on their doors with enough force to split the wood.

Then again, the king didn't often summon palace guests to his private study for late night conversation. As Marco stared at his father, it occurred to him that the king's early morning appearance likely had to do with Amanda Hutton.

"Father?" Marco opened the door wide. "What's going on?"

The king looked Marco up and down, his eyebrows raised in disapproval. "Perhaps I should allow you to dress first. Do you often answer your door in your nightwear?"

"I do at this hour."

Eduardo shook his head in irritation, but strode past Marco into the sitting room. "Your predilection for responses like that, my son, is what I am here to discuss. Among other things."

Marco bit back an even more sarcastic reply. The king lifted the edge of a plush gray curtain to look out the sitting room window as dawn swept over the garden below, then allowed the fabric to fall before taking a seat in one of Marco's black leather chairs. He gestured to a matching seat. "Come, Marco. We have important matters to discuss this morning."

Marco closed the door, forced his irritation from his expression, then crossed the room to join his father. After dropping into his favorite chair, he put his bare feet on the coffee table to his father's obvious displeasure.

"Marco."

Marco eyed his father, challenging him to make a comment. He was a grown man in his own apartment. If he felt like wearing a robe and putting his feet on the furniture in the early morning hours, before the rest of the world rolled out of bed, even the king shouldn't object.

"Marco," Eduardo repeated, his tone slightly more conciliatory this time. "I shall get right to the point. I disapprove of the cavalier attitude you've displayed since your return to the palace."

Deciding his best course of action was to remain silent, Marco waited.

"What you do in your own apartment," the king gestured toward Marco's feet as the prince shifted them on the table, "is your concern. However, once you walk out the door, your actions are my concern."

When Marco again opted to remain silent, the king rose, returning to the large window that overlooked the palace garden. "You're beginning to acquire a reputation, Marco. When you were in the military, I assumed you chose to jump out of planes and accept risky assignments because you thought it noble, or because you wanted to enjoy such escapades before committing to a more sedate public service role here at La Rocca. I allowed you to do so, despite the fact a prince must be more cautious than other soldiers, given his value to society."

The king exhaled, and Marco didn't like what he saw in the set of his father's shoulders. "But now, you are taking those same risks in your private activities. You fail to consider the ramifications of your behavior on others."

Marco raised an eyebrow. "I haven't heard any complaints."

"You wouldn't. But I have. For instance, when I taught you to ski, I told you how important it is to set a moderate pace, to stop and smile at those who recognize you. To pause for photographers. But instead, I understand that you are reckless. You ski too fast, you ignore everyone but your friends. It does not leave a good impression."

"I'm not reckless. I'm *good*. And with my helmet on and a little speed, few people recognize me."

The king slammed his hand against the window ledge, then turned to face Marco. "You're more recognizable than you believe. My advisors are becoming concerned about the talk. In some of our social circles, there is speculation about the amount you gamble. And about the number of women you see."

A gambler, maybe. And only with his private money, never his state allowance. But a complaint about women? Just because they pursued him whenever he went out in public didn't mean he'd done anything untoward. He'd never so much as touched them.

"Wait a minute," he asked, suddenly suspicious. "Is this about

Amanda Hutton?" Maybe his father had seen their exchange in the garden after all. If so, he'd set the man straight immediately.

The king frowned. "As a matter of fact, it is. How did you know?"

Marco hesitated. His father looked a little too surprised by his reference to Amanda. "How did I know *what*, exactly?"

"That I've hired her?"

A knot formed in Marco's stomach as he realized the mistaken assumption he'd made. And what his father must have done. "You hired her?" he asked. "To do what?"

"To act as your tutor, I suppose you would call it. She is to guide you in all matters of protocol, to help you find your niche in public life."

"A tutor."

"A coach, if you prefer that term. Or an advisor."

Marco pulled his feet from the coffee table and straightened. "I appreciate that you want me to be more comfortable in the palace, but I'm an adult. A *tutor* certainly isn't necessary." He hadn't wanted to take this final step but, Marco supposed, in his gut he'd always known he would. He barreled on, "Besides, I'm only going to be here at the palace temporarily. I've decided that it would be best for me to re-enlist. I know it's not a very public role, but I would be serving the people of San—"

"No."

"No?" His chin jerked involuntarily, as if his father had punched him.

"No. You are needed here. There are simply too many demands on my time. I must be able to delegate certain tasks to other members of the family."

Marco clenched his teeth to keep his jaw from dropping open. He'd always thought his father would approve if he opted for a career in the military. It wasn't his dream job, but it was a hell of a lot more comfortable than remaining in the cold fishbowl of public life at the palace. And other choices, choices that appealed to him—managing a ski resort or an expedition company, for instance—simply weren't possible for him as a prince.

"Father," Marco took care not to directly contradict his father, "surely Antony, Federico, and Isabella can handle anything you must delegate. Antony is a very popular speaker. He's an ace at handling social dinners and knowledgeable on foreign affairs. Federico did a very effective job at last month's economic summit, and Isabella has proven herself time and time again—"

"This is not up for discussion, Marco. You will not return to the military."

The king sighed, then approached and placed a hand on Marco's shoulder. His tone softened, though his commanding gaze did not. "There are thousands who can take on your military role, but only you can fulfill your role as prince. You can be more effective in that role than you believe. You are a caring, intelligent man. People who know you personally are incredibly loyal to you, and they respect you."

His grip tightened on Marco's shoulder for a fraction of a second. "I'm proud of who you are, and I want you to live up to your potential. That means remaining here and becoming an active force in this household."

He dropped his hand from Marco's shoulder and strode toward the door, leaving no opportunity for argument. He paused before opening it to say, "Ms. Hutton will meet with you in the library in one hour. Be dressed appropriately and ready to learn. Above all, do not blame her for my decision. Allow her to do her job. I will give you complete privacy, and I expect you to use the time well. You are scheduled with her for daily sessions and you will not miss them. Understood?"

"Yes, sir." He understood, all right. He was getting a tutor whether he wanted one or not. And *complete privacy.* For hours, day after day, with exactly the kind of woman he'd sworn he'd never allow into his life.

Marco closed his eyes. How could he possibly handle seeing Amanda in such intimate circumstances after what had passed between them last night? His head swam, forcing him to press the heel of his hand to his forehead. His palm stung where the rose's thorn had pierced his flesh earlier, which only added to his frustration.

"And Marco," the king waited for Marco's attention before shooting his son a final, stern look, "you are not to leave the palace grounds until your term with Ms. Hutton is complete. Not without my express prior permission."

"My term? Like a jail sentence?" Marco rose from the chair. He'd kept his resentment in check thus far, but for his father to keep him under what amounted to house arrest was too much. "And just how long do you expect this 'term' to run? I have plans—"

"As long as it takes. Cancel your other plans. I am quite serious about this."

Marco flung his arms wide. "And I am quite capable of handling my own affairs. Perhaps I don't wish to cancel—"

The king's face turned to stone. "I am not merely your father, Marco. I am your king. You would do well to remember that on occasion."

"Sir—"

"If you wish to leave the palace, you shall find you lack transportation."

With that, the king left, the door closing behind him with a firm click as the mechanism slid into place.

"Damn it all," Marco muttered to the silent room. He stared at the door for a moment, then paced the sitting room as his anger boiled over.

So much for the hiking trip. So much for avoiding crowded, fusty palace functions. And so much for staying away from *her*.

He stopped pacing and ran his hands over his head. He needed to take a long, cool shower. Then he'd think of an escape plan.

No way was he going to submit to etiquette lessons—especially lessons with Amanda Hutton—without a fight.

CHAPTER 5

MARCO HESITATED outside the double doors to the library. After a quick, reinforcing breath, he peeked around the corner.

With her usual model-perfect posture, Amanda perched on the edge of the chair behind his great-grandmother's cherry writing desk, giving him a clear view of her profile. Blessedly oblivious to his presence, Amanda creased her forehead in concentration and ran the index finger of her left hand down a sheet of paper. Every few seconds, she mumbled something to herself, then read on.

He gritted his teeth. Probably a long list of his shortcomings, courtesy of King Eduardo.

He wondered for a moment if she would find as much fault with him as his family did. Judging from her rigid carriage and pristine, coffee-colored silk suit, she appeared ready to play the part of royal tutor—*advisor*, he corrected himself—particularly given that he recognized the suit as one belonging to his sister, Princess Isabella.

Great. If his sister had helped Amanda, loaning her professional clothing until her own arrived from the States, no doubt his brothers had also heard of the hasty arrangements. Would his family ever learn to respect him as an adult?

Marco eased back into the hallway, out of Amanda's line of sight, and took a moment to temper his anger. He twirled the now-open yellow rose between his fingers, knowing he had to address what had happened between them the night before and make it seem like nothing. Family meddling or not, if he could get it through his skull that the woman had *uptight* written all over her, that he had been imagining things when he'd sensed a mutual attraction, he should be able to pull off his plan.

One thing he'd learned in the military: don't go into a conflict swinging. Discover all you can about your enemy, then use that knowledge to your advantage. In this instance, he had to consider Amanda the enemy, even if the enemy possessed the legs of a Vegas showgirl and a smile that made his body respond whether he wanted it to or not.

He stole another quick glance into the library. Amanda had twisted in the seat, apparently to check the time on the grandfather clock in the far corner.

His mouth quirked in satisfaction. So far, his plan ran as expected. He was late, and as he'd guessed, Amanda Hutton was the type who demanded her world run with the same precision as the well-oiled clock. She followed the rules, appreciated order, civility, and, above all, promptness.

Given all that, he reminded himself, she probably didn't find him the least bit appealing. After all, *he'd* kissed *her* in the garden. She hadn't kissed back. She'd left his flower behind without a thought.

Then she'd agreed to work for his father.

He ruffled his already-unkempt hair. He could make this work. Had to make this work. He'd concluded during his shower that getting around the tutoring arrangement itself was impossible. Even if Amanda bolted from the job, the king would inevitably find someone else to take her place. Eduardo wasn't an easily dissuaded man once he set his mind to something.

But Marco could ensure that hire wouldn't be Amanda Hutton. Amanda had affected his psyche, and whether she was attracted to him or not, he couldn't allow himself to become emotionally attached to her. He'd learned that lesson the hard way.

After checking his watch to ensure he'd waited at least ten minutes past their appointed meeting time, he scrutinized his clothes. Damn the valet who'd pressed his pants. He looked as if he'd taken time with his appearance, just as his father expected, but no way in hell was he entering that room looking like a schoolboy ready to sit quietly and absorb his daily lessons. He was twenty-five, for crying out loud. A college graduate. A former army officer.

He yanked on his pant legs, crushing the fabric in his hands. No dice. Settling for a half-untucked shirt, he strode into the library.

Amanda looked up from the desk as he approached. Once again, her luminous hazel eyes made his breath hitch in his throat, despite the fact she glared at him as if he'd gone truant.

"Good morning, Your Highness. I was about to come looking for you...again. King Eduardo insisted we begin at eight a.m. sharp. You're twelve minutes late." She gestured to his clothing. "And you should tuck in your shirt. I expect my students to arrive as if they were about to meet someone of importance, since that's the focus of my instruction."

AMANDA FORCED herself to keep her hands still and her breath steady as Marco diTalora met her stare with a lopsided smile. She'd been up half the night, internally debating the best way to adapt her lessons to suit an adult client—an adult client who'd kissed her, and would have done far more had his father not interrupted. At about four in the morning, she gave up and opted to wing it. From what she'd seen, Marco diTalora was a man who enjoyed action, so he'd probably rebuff the classroom tactics she employed with her usual students.

Her suspicions were confirmed by Princess Isabella, who'd stopped by her room around seven with coffee and an offer to lend Amanda a few outfits until her own clothing arrived from home. Isabella had actually laughed when Amanda asked whether Marco might prefer an open lesson plan to something more structured. But the princess warned her that she couldn't appear too lax, or Marco would run right over her.

From the prince's appearance this morning, Amanda knew she'd have her work cut out for her.

Though Marco appeared freshly showered and shaved, his hair had returned to the tousled, surfer-boy look he'd sported the previous afternoon at the casino. Not exactly the look of a man ready to take her instruction seriously.

And he looked a bit too happy to see her.

He tucked in his shirt with a hint of amusement in his eyes, then jammed one hand into the pocket of his tailored black slacks and leaned against the rich, red brocade-covered wall opposite the desk.

"A pleasure to see you again so soon, Ms. Hutton." A slow, sexy smile spread across the perfect planes of his face. "I understand my father hired you to teach me which fork to use."

She leaned back in her chair, studying him. Their last encounter had been breathtakingly intimate, yet given the circumstances, he shouldn't be at all happy to see her.

Careful to choose the right words, she answered, "I thought we had this conversation yesterday in the car. As you might recall, I told you that what I do goes far beyond forks."

"Funny you should mention that." He took a few steps toward her, displaying the same devil-may-care attitude he'd exhibited as they'd left the casino. The one that said he knew he was a good-looking prince and wanted to work his magic on her. To her shock, he produced the yellow rose she'd dropped on the garden path. Had he been hiding it behind his back?

He tossed the rose to the desktop and continued, "Given what happened in the garden last night, and the fact that my father has now ordered us to spend ungodly amounts of private time together, I suspect we could go *far* beyond—"

"Don't even think about it." Amanda stood, placing her hands on the desk to keep them from shaking. His all-too-at-ease demeanor made perfect sense now.

Given what she knew of his reputation, what had passed between them last night had been out of the ordinary for him—enough that he'd kept the rose she'd left behind—and had given her a brief insight into his complex soul. Still, Prince Marco was a rogue, a rascal, a prankster. Jennifer and Isabella had both warned her of that, and she'd come to the library prepared.

Apparently—she forced herself not to look at the flower on the desk—so had he.

If she wanted to keep this job, she could not to succumb to his charms, either the deeply personal emotion she'd glimpsed when he'd kissed her wrist in the garden, or the purposeful advances he made now.

He slipped around the desk to stand within arm's reach, rested his rear against the polished surface, then slowly leaned forward to whisper near her ear, "And just what am I thinking, Ms. Hutton?"

His warm breath caressed her cheek, and for the briefest moment, she thought about turning toward him, seeing if he would give her a real kiss this time. Would the reality hold up to the promise of fun and adventure of his easy smiles?

Instead, she straightened, ignoring the pull she always felt in his presence, and lifted her chin to look him in the eye. "You're thinking you can get out of your lessons by flirting with me. That either I'll quit for the sake of propriety, or your father will think something's fishy and fire me. Either way, it won't work."

She circled the chair, putting a safe distance between herself and Prince Charming.

Instead of pursuing her or even arguing with her, he tossed back his head and laughed. Crossing his arms over his chest, he asked, "Am I that transparent? What gave me away?"

Unable to keep from returning his grin, she put a little more space between them and explained, "Nothing in particular. My students will usually try anything they can to get out of lessons, especially the first day." She waved a hand toward the desk, dismissing the importance of the rose as he now seemed willing to do. "Of course, I've never had any of them try...well, *that* one on me before. Then again, my students have always been at least a decade younger than you are."

She eased herself into one of the library's yellow silk chairs. "In any case, as I said, it won't work. The king wants you to become part of the palace social and political scene. I'm to work with you until you're comfortable in that role. From what he's told me, you'll be a willing pupil."

His brows lifted. "My father can be convincing when he wants his children to do something. What I can't understand is why you took the job."

"As you said, your father is a convincing man."

"Quite." He levered his hips from the desk, then approached and took the chair beside hers. She could see in his eyes that he still wanted to propose they forget the whole thing.

"And," she added hastily, in case he intended to flirt with her again, "I'm not much of a risk-taker. As you might guess, going against your father's wishes could pose a great risk to someone in my occupation. You're stuck with me."

His eyes glittered with mischief. "Now we're getting down to it. What did my father hold over your head?"

"Your father didn't hold anything over my head," she said. "Lesson number one: it's not particularly polite to insinuate that I've done something he could hold over me."

Well, King Eduardo hadn't blackmailed her. But she hadn't exactly been able to say no, either.

"I'm sure I do impolite things all the time, Ms. Hutton, which is why my father hired you. But I didn't mean to imply that there's anything shady in your past. Perhaps he convinced you for another reason?"

"I'm a professional. It's not as if I need convincing to do my job."

"Children are your job."

"We all need something new and different on occasion. A challenge." She certainly wasn't going to tell Marco she was hard up for cash. He'd probably hand her a wad of bills and arrange an immediate car service to the airport.

He lifted his gaze to the ceiling for a moment, then grinned. "A challenge. You know, my family has described me that way more than once. But I can tell from your expression that you had other reasons to take the job. Perhaps if you tell me what they are, I can work out an arrangement that suits us both."

"What do you mean, an arrangement?"

"No personal offense to you, Ms. Hutton, but despite my failed attempt to get you to quit, I have no intention of being tutored as if I were in primary school."

Amanda's breakfast churned in her stomach. She couldn't lose this job the first day. She'd be out the money, as well as the king's recommendation for her next job. It'd also sting her pride.

He edged close to her once again, and she caught a faint whiff of his cologne. He smelled as delicious as he had when they'd walked side by side through the narrow casino hallway.

"Why do you need this job? Is it merely the challenge, or something else? Prestige? Money?"

When he hit on the answer, it must have shown on her face because his grin went as wide as the Cheshire Cat's. "Ah, I see. Money. I imagine he offered you quite a bit."

"You're unconscionably rude. We'll work on that."

"It's not for the money?"

"Of course not." She waved a hand at the rich trappings around them. "But you of all people must admit, Your Highness, that money can help you get what you want in life. You wouldn't be able to spend nearly so much time gambling or out boating if not for your wealth and position."

"If not for my wealth and position, perhaps I wouldn't feel the need."

His blue-eyed stare seemed to go right through her. She didn't have a response.

After several beats, he asked, "What is it you want in life, Amanda? If you had my money, I mean."

"Independence," she said, then instantly regretted it. Here she was, someone who taught the elite how to rein in their emotions, how to keep their personal lives private when put on the spot, and she'd just revealed her deepest fear to him: that she'd never be completely free of her father's influence, or his disappointment if she failed.

Prince Marco had a gift for knocking her off balance.

"And that's all I want." His tone was surprisingly sincere. He gestured to the official portrait of King Eduardo that dominated the far wall of the library. "As you can imagine, my father likes to keep his offspring in check. Skiing, boating, the rush of air against my face, the blessed absence of anyone judging me or telling me what to do...did you ever consider that gives me a feeling of freedom I can't have while I'm trapped in this ancient mausoleum of a palace?"

She blew out a long breath. She did understand. Maybe, if he saw that, she could turn her own struggle into a strength.

"My father was once the American ambassador to Italy," she began. "He's currently an advisor to the president. His position doesn't compare to that of your father, but it does mean that he's used to power. And he tends to wield that power over members of his own family."

Marco's eyes danced. "You're trying to free yourself, the same as I am."

She shifted in her chair. "In a way. But while I understand the frustration of being a born into a prominent family, I wasn't born into a job, as you were. Your father is also your head of state, while my father holds no political power over me. Even so, neither of us can change the circumstances of our birth, and it's my job to help you live within that framework."

"And if you lose that job? Or quit? Do you lose your independence?"

"You could look at it that way," she conceded as she smoothed her skirt. The borrowed clothing only served to remind her that, in a way, she was on borrowed time. "If I left this position without lining up another, I'd be hard put to pay the rent on my apartment as well as cover the expenses necessary for my business. Maintaining my own residence and my own business are what give me a sense of independence."

Even as the words left her mouth, her brain wondered why she was telling Prince Marco all of this. The whole adult-as-student frontier was new to her, and she hadn't come prepared, particularly for this adult student. She smiled, hoping to salvage the mess she'd talked herself into. "My personal life isn't the issue, though. We need to focus on you and what you need to flourish and find the sense of freedom you crave, given your unique circumstances. I wanted you to know I understand that this isn't your choice, and I empathize."

Marco considered that for a moment, then rose from his chair and strode to the window. He stared out at the garden, and she wondered if he saw his father—the king was known to regularly jog along its pathways in the morning—and what thoughts were going through his head.

Finally, Marco turned to face her. "I admit, I came here this morning with the single goal of convincing you to quit. But even if you refused the arrangement I originally proposed" —he shot an openly approving look at her legs, causing her instantly to tuck them under her chair— "another type of arrangement might work. Perhaps what we need is an alliance."

MARCO RAN his palm along the cool window frame. As much as he hated giving in, perhaps he'd made a mistake in judgment. Amanda, for all the danger she posed to him, wasn't the enemy in this situation. His father was.

Her eyes narrowed. "What do you mean, an alliance?"

"Think about the essence of our situation. If my father is displeased with you, you're out a job and your independence. If he's displeased with my progress, my freedom gets cut even more than it is now. But if we work together, we both get what we want."

"What is it you're proposing? Keeping in mind, of course, that I have no intention of breaking my word to your father." She recrossed her legs as she spoke, and he forced himself keep his chin lifted so he didn't appear to follow the movement.

"I'm not asking you to. I think it's in both of our best interests to get these lessons, or whatever you like to call what we're doing, over as quickly as possible. That way you can move on to your next position with a glowing recommendation from my father to open the door, and I can have my life back." To a limited extent, anyway. His father had made it clear he'd be part of the palace scene from now on, but at least he'd be able to leave the grounds.

She cocked her head. "I'm listening."

"I'll be a willing, obedient student, given some basic ground rules."

"Such as?"

"First, I expect to be treated as an adult. No lectures about my shirt hanging out or other appearance-related issues. I realize you're used to teaching kids, but I know how I'm supposed to look when it's important. You might note that I was in perfect form for the wedding. Not to mention that I fixed your dress in the car to keep *you* from appearing wrinkled."

Though her gaze didn't waver, color rose in her cheeks, giving him a flash of satisfaction. "Fine. And?"

"You call me Marco. None of this 'Your Highness' business when we're alone. And if it's all right, I'd prefer to call you Amanda."

She shook her head. "You may call me Amanda, but it doesn't show respect for a commoner to call a prince by his first name."

"You'll drive me insane."

"How about Prince Marco? It's not quite as formal as 'Your Highness.' Good enough compromise?"

He made a small rumble of protest. "No, but I suppose I'll survive."

"You'll survive. Well, that's good to hear, Prince Marco. Otherwise, I'd have a hard time explaining your sudden death to your father. Is that it for ground rules?"

He couldn't help but grin. "For now. We can figure out the rest as we go along."

He noticed her glance at the clock, ever vigilant to the passage of time. "All right, since it's getting late, let's begin with lesson one."

"How to escape the palace buzzards in three easy steps?"

"That's a temporary fix. You need long term solutions," Amanda said, shooting him a disciplinary frown that reminded him of one his mother had given him when he was around eight years old, upon discovering he'd substituted tiny balls of green Play-Doh for the peas on her plate at a state dinner.

He pushed the memory aside and waved off Amanda's staid attitude. If they were going to be in tight quarters for the foreseeable future, she'd have to learn to deal with his sense of humor, just as his mother had. While Queen Aletta hadn't appreciated his stunt, she'd later admitted that the dignitary being honored that evening might have benefitted from a taste of Play-Doh.

Amanda started to say something, then hesitated for a moment, as if sizing him up. Finally, she angled her head in the general direction of the garden. "You were uncomfortable at the wedding reception. Why?"

Blunt. The woman was far too blunt. And intuitive.

"Be honest," she added.

He gave a self-effacing shrug. "Paparazzi, I suppose. They're annoying. And nosy. I think they'd make anyone uncomfortable."

"There weren't any paparazzi around when you invited me to go for a walk," she pointed out. "The few press photographers at the reception were only permitted to stay for the first hour. I had the distinct impression you were avoiding Eliza Schipani and the parliament member she was talking to."

"They're nosy, too."

Her hazel eyes filled with amusement. "Perhaps. But why the need for escape? If they were getting personal, why not just tell them to butt out? In a diplomatic way, of course."

That was the crux of the problem. No matter what he did, people he barely knew always seemed to twist the conversation to his personal life, and he could never figure out how to respond.

"It's difficult," he finally answered. "I'm not a conversationalist."

She raised a brow. "You do fine with me. When we left the casino, you were quite comfortable telling me exactly what words I should be using to compliment your tux."

"That's different," he argued, embarrassed now to remember he'd used the lines on her he usually reserved for the daft women who pursued him around town. "It was only the two of us. No cameras, no reporters."

"It's not that different at all. You used humor to change the topic, to keep me distracted from the fact I was angry that I had to comb the casinos hunting you down."

He eased away from the windowsill. "Listen, I'm sorry about that—"

"It's forgotten," she said. "My point is, you have the basic skills. You need to get comfortable using them in a different environment. A more formal one. You might not be as unguarded with Eliza Schipani or a parliament member as you were with your friends, or with me yesterday, but you'll take the same approach."

"So when someone like Eliza dogs me for hours about having me speak at her health conference—"

"You kindly accept."

"You haven't heard a word I said."

Her mouth twisted into a wry smile. "Of course I have. You told me you don't like public events. It's my job to make you comfortable with them."

"But what if I don't want to accept a particular invitation, like Eliza's? Say I'm booked elsewhere." Like on a ski trip.

"Then you thank her and say you're booked elsewhere. *If* you're truly booked."

He paced the room for a minute, considering Amanda's words. The sensation of her eyes tracking his every move unnerved him. "So how do you propose I become comfortable in public situations? Without making a fool of myself, I mean."

"Practice. We'll run through some scenarios here, mock receptions, that sort of thing. I'll see how you handle yourself, give you some guidelines for use in the real world. Then we'll try them out in public." His hesitancy must have shown, because she continued, "Don't worry. I'll start you out with something simple, in an arena that's relatively comfortable for you. Tell me, what kind of things do you like to do?" A smile lit her face as she added, "Besides gamble."

He ticked a few items off on his fingers. "Ski. Hike. Race boats.

Spend time with my friends." He let his hand drop to his side. "Trust me, there's not a public event that gets me excited."

"Wrong time of year for skiing." He could almost see the wheels of her mind spinning. "A boat race is possible. Yes. We'll make your return to public life here in San Rimini a boat race."

He shot her a skeptical look. "If we have to. What's the catch?"

"Well, I'd like to get you in a real-life situation as soon as possible. Two weeks, if we can manage it."

He tamped down the instant wave of horror that rose in his chest. "There are three or four races in San Rimini each year, but none of the invitations on my assistant's desk involve—"

"No, I meant I want you *hosting* an event in less than two weeks. A boat race could raise quite a bit of money for a charitable cause. A perfectly appropriate event for a prince to host."

Her eyes sparkled as if she'd hit upon a brilliant idea and was completely settled on it. Rising from her chair, she moved to the desk, then turned so her back was to it and her hips rested against the desktop. She braced her palms on either side of her, then drummed her fingers, as if she could hardly contain herself.

Either Amanda was incredibly confident in her own skills or she didn't understand the limitations of his.

"You want me to host a charity boat race in two weeks? No way."

"My job is to make you at ease in your role as a prince. That role necessarily means hosting certain events. Now, I could start you out with a state dinner if any are planned in the—"

"No, never, no."

"Which is why what I'm suggesting—or something like it—would be more appropriate." She had him where she wanted him, and he could tell by her confident expression that she knew it. "It's less political, not so high-profile. If you make a mistake, we can both learn from it and move on, though I'll do my best to ensure no mistakes are made."

"Trust me, when I'm piloting a speedboat, no mistakes—"

"And that brings us to the catch," she cut in. "We couldn't possibly host the kind of race you envision in such short order. There are liability issues, for one thing. Second, we'd have to block off a sizable area of San Rimini Bay for such an event, which requires permits. Even getting entrants in that time span would be difficult."

"So what do you propose?"

"Well, I attended this duck race in Washington, D.C., a couple of years ago—"

"A...duck race?"

"Of a sort. I think we can use the same approach here."

Marco groaned and forked his fingers into his hair. He didn't want her to explain. Just using the word *duck* meant he'd look like an idiot after all.

"Your Highness—"

"Marco!" he barked. He shook his head, then crossed the room to rest his hips on the desk beside hers. He heaved out a breath, acknowledging that his tone was out of line, but that he wasn't happy with the situation.

"Prince Marco." Her voice was low and soothing. She reached across the short distance between them to cover his hand with hers. She gave it a quick squeeze, then pulled away before he could think about it. "Remember, we're in this together. Both of us have our reputations on the line. You proposed an alliance, so you're going to have to trust me."

He trusted her. He wasn't so sure he trusted himself, particularly if she gave him reassuring pats on the hand or arm.

He gave her a sidelong glance. "Ducks?"

"Ducks. We'll start today. By event time, you'll be fine."

He had serious doubts. Then again, it wasn't as if he had a choice.

CHAPTER 6

AMANDA LET her mind relax for the first time in more than two weeks as she absorbed the sights and sounds of the Adriatic from the royal family's private pier.

Behind her, the pier stretched to kiss the shoreline at the foot of the elegant Palazzo d'Avorio, a fortress built from local ivory-colored stone nearly five hundred years earlier to guard the entrance to San Rimini Bay. In the early days of his reign, King Eduardo had renovated the structure to serve as both a functional boathouse and seaside entertainment facility. With its spacious banquet rooms upstairs and modern kitchen and storage areas below, at the water's edge, it was the obvious site to host Marco's charity event.

The gentle blue waves of the bay lapped a safe distance beneath Amanda's toes, coaxing her to look past her new pedicure and through the spaces between the pier's wooden slats. Brilliantly colored fish darted from pylon to pylon, and a lone chunk of seaweed floated with the tide.

"The water is so clear, even close to shore," she marveled to Marco, who stood beside her. "It's a beautiful day. Couldn't have asked for better."

Shading her eyes, she gazed out to sea and took in a lungful of the salty air. The sun beat down on her shoulders, warming both her body and her spirits. She and Prince Marco had arrived early to double check the arrangements and, finding that the staff had outdone themselves, decided to take a quick walk on the pier before the first guests arrived for pre-race hors d'oeuvres and cocktails.

She remained as incomprehensibly attracted to him as when they'd met, but she'd taken care in their sessions to keep things professional. It had become easier once the rose he'd clipped in the garden finally died. After he'd brought it to their first meeting, she'd taken it back to her room and put it in water.

Not having to see it on her bedside table each night kept her from thinking about their time in the garden. At least, she didn't think about it quite as often.

"I was counting on rain," Marco said in a mock grumble beside her.

"In San Rimini? At this time of year? Fat chance."

He shrugged. "Probably for the best. I'd hate to have to return the donations."

Amanda smiled inwardly. They'd been able to organize the charity event in only sixteen days. Given Prince Marco's name as host on the invitations—a first that caused RSVPs to hit his assistant's inbox mere hours after the invitations left the palace—he was certain to raise a good deal of money for the San Riminian Cancer Council. Despite his grousing about rain, Amanda knew Marco wasn't worried about the event being a financial success.

He needed it to be a personal success.

She tore her gaze from the picturesque sea to face him. Despite spending two long weeks trying to ignore his obvious sex appeal, forcing herself to keep at least an arm's distance from him at all times, his very presence still stole her breath.

The paparazzi, gathered a stone's throw away along the seaside road leading to the Palazzo d'Avorio, wouldn't notice anything unusual about him as they stared through their oversized camera lenses. A white polo shirt skimmed his broad shoulders to emphasize the muscles in his chest. Crisp, lightweight beige slacks accentuated his lean skier's hips and athletic legs, and his designer sunglasses seemed selected to show the planes of his face in the best possible manner. With his easy stance and a half smile tugging at the edges of his full lips, he appeared exactly as one expected: a self-assured young royal prepared to host a casual charity event.

Under his polished exterior, however, she suspected Marco had a case of nerves to rival those of a high-school girl waiting for her prom date to arrive...fifteen minutes after that date was supposed to show.

"You'll do fine, Prince Marco." Despite the fact he hadn't mentioned his intense dislike of public gatherings since their first day together, she felt the need to reassure him. He could do this. She knew he could. He'd kept true to his word, making it to each of their scheduled sessions on time. Though he'd balked at several of the exercises, he'd completed each one. They'd practiced dicey conversations with each of them taking turns in his role, while the other would pretend to be a reporter, a palace guest, a parliament member, or even a child on the street during a family meet-and-greet.

"These are all scenarios you're likely to experience," she'd reminded him. "Over the coming years, you'll participate in a range of events, from touring hospitals to visiting schools to attending high society dinners where people truly do care about which fork you use. The more you practice, the easier each situation will become." She'd also given him links to a dozen websites that offered information on current events, and asked him to read through those with which he was unfamiliar. "You won't be quizzed," she'd told him. "But it's good to have a basic grasp on what's happening so you can speak with confidence. Even a bare knowledge will allow you to acknowledge the speaker and then ask about their thoughts."

"Turn the burden of the conversation back to them," he'd said. "Make it easy to keep myself from committing to a particular political stance or opinion."

"Exactly."

Hopefully, now that the first event had arrived, the lessons had taken root.

"I know, I know. You keep telling me I'm ready," he said, then mimicked her voice, "Trust me!"

She smiled at the imitation. "It won't be as bad as you imagine. Compared to the state dinners Prince Antony and your father regularly host, this afternoon will be a breeze."

"I suppose that's something to be thankful for." He shifted as he looked out to sea. "I doubt conversation stays focused on the race. Around me, anyway. Most of those who accepted the invitation care about two things: furthering their personal political agendas and gathering as much royal gossip as they can so they'll have something to chatter about at their next party."

He flicked a crust of bread he'd filched from one of the hors d'oeuvres trays to a nearby seagull. As the bird swooped from the sky to grab the treat, Marco added, "I'll do my best, but I'm bound to put my foot in my mouth before the afternoon is over. I always do at these events."

"Today is a new start. Think of how you did yesterday. I tried to pin you on a number of topics, and you did wonderfully."

"Role playing isn't the real thing."

"It's close enough. Even so, I'll try to stay within view. If you need me to bail you out of an awkward situation, put a hand in your front pocket."

The prince watched as the seagull veered toward the crowd onshore, apparently deciding Marco had no more tidbits to offer. "Put a hand in my pocket. Right. Even if you do manage to politely insert yourself into the discussion, I doubt you'd be able to stop an egotistical parliament member from prying into my family's personal affairs. Or fishing for information about the pending economic agreement with Greece. The Greek minister arrives tomorrow, and there are a lot of people who want to know all the details before they're finalized and an announcement is made." Marco screwed up his face. "Nothing stops the really determined ones from grilling me, even when it's a topic I'm not knowledgeable about. Perhaps especially then. I think they get a thrill from proving they know more than I do."

"Maybe, but never forget that you're a prince. If they're socially savvy, they'll follow your lead."

He parroted her voice, "If the conversation is headed in a direction that makes you uncomfortable, try to change the subject. Keep at least two safe topics of conversation in mind at all times."

She raised a warning finger in jest. "But stay away from the weather. Nothing's more boring."

"This from the woman who was just telling me what a beautiful day it is."

"Hey—"

"I'm kidding." He took off his sunglasses, inspected the lenses, then rubbed them against his shirt to remove a tiny speck of dirt, an uncharacteristic bit of self-awareness that gave away his unsettled thoughts. "Seriously, though, what if changing the topic doesn't work?"

"Refer them to your father if it's political. If they're pressing you about a social event, postpone by saying you have to check with your assistant. And you can always play dumb if someone doesn't take the hint."

He replaced his now-clean sunglasses. "Can't. Dumb's too hard on the ego."

"A few seconds of silence, then. Allow *them* to be uncomfortable. If it comes to that, it's their fault, not yours. They will be the person who pushed the conversation too far. Then make another attempt to change the topic."

He grimaced, and Amanda could see him running through possibilities in his head.

"One last piece of advice?"

"I suppose you'll tell me, whether I want to hear it or not."

"Don't make faces like that." She tilted her head. "The paparazzi are snapping away over there. That look you just gave me could end up on the cover of a magazine. Or at least on a gossip site."

He grinned for the first time since their arrival nearly a half hour earlier, giving her a flash of white teeth. "You have to admit, that wouldn't be the worst coverage I've ever had."

"For today, we're keeping it positive. It's good for you, and good for the cause." She checked her watch. "Time to head in. The first guests will be here any minute."

He lowered his voice and made the sound of a church bell tolling out doom.

If not for his title and the cameras, she'd have punched him on the arm. "What did I just say about staying positive?"

He bowed at the waist, gesturing her ahead of him on the pier. "After you, my lady."

"Forget what I said about playing dumb. Just do that."

"Do what?"

"Be your charming self."

He straightened, his quiet laugh barely audible over the scream of a nearby seagull and the lapping of the waves against the pier.

"Charming. Now that I've always been able to pull off."

MARCO FEARED his spinal cord would give out any minute. All day mogul skiing? Tiring, but no problem. Hiking over a long weekend in Switzerland? Piece of cake. But how long could a man stand with perfect posture, acting as if he had a rod inserted from his tailbone to his skull? Let alone grin like a fool as an endless stream of millionaires, government officials, and celebrities cornered him to speculate aloud on inane topics.

He angled his head and did his best to feign interest as the white-haired socialite in front of him droned on about the San Rimini Garden Society's latest rose show. He loved roses and could listen to an expert discuss their horticulture all day, but this woman's complaints about the display booth setup left him glassy-eyed. He prayed he didn't look as bored as he felt.

Why his father thought it was important for him to do this when Antony, Federico, and Isabella not only excelled at it but seemed to enjoy it, was quite beyond him. Certainly he could make other contributions to the family.

Like the boat race itself. Of course, if it could be a *real* boat race...

Tempted to massage his aching neck, he decided instead to occupy his hands with a glass of champagne taken from the tray of a passing waiter. He sipped slowly as he listened to the woman before him chatter on, and discreetly scanned the room for Amanda.

He'd resisted spending time with her in the beginning, certain there was no point in her advice, but had to admit that her instruction had made this afternoon bearable. Twice he'd evaded questions about the pending economic agreement, and he'd done so without feeling awkward or sounding as if he wanted to dodge the subject. And, thanks to Amanda's boat race idea, he would be able to spend most of the afternoon outside in the fresh air instead of trapped in a corner listening to people like the Garden Lady.

Chalk up two points for Amanda Hutton.

After the Garden Lady took her leave, he made a slow circle through the banquet hall—complimenting one of his distant cousins on her new hairstyle, then offering congratulations to one of San Rimini's professional tennis players on making the semifinals of the previous year's French Open—all the while keeping his eyes peeled for Amanda. She'd promised to stay within sight, hadn't she?

For the last two weeks, he'd struggled to keep her at a safe distance, with the desk or a coffee table between them whenever possible. Just far enough away to keep from accidentally brushing up against her or breathing in the scent of her shampoo. It had taken all his will to resist the urge to reach out for her, to see if she'd return a kiss if he gave her another.

Of course, now that he really needed her, she was nowhere in sight.

Finally, he noticed her standing next to one of the hall's floor-to-ceiling windows, her gaze following a pair of motorboats as they bumped along the waves of San Rimini Bay. With her polished ponytail hanging neatly down her back and a pair of tasteful but inexpensive sunglasses perched atop her head, she looked ready for a day on the water herself.

He smiled to himself as he watched her watch the boats, considering the absurdity of the event she'd proposed. When this was over, he'd have to treat her to a real boat race. One that made her pulse pound and dampened her face with saltwater spray.

He started toward her, chatting as briefly as possible with guests as he went. He paused to grab a glass of champagne for Amanda, but stopped short when Viscount Renati, a close friend of Antony's, apparently had the same idea. The young viscount approached Amanda with two champagne flutes, proffering one when she looked up. She'd apparently been expecting him, because she took the glass without hesitation and started chatting as if they were old friends.

"Angelo Renati." Marco rolled the name over on his tongue, then watched as the viscount brushed an invisible piece of lint from the sleeve of Amanda's navy blue dress.

Despite being a close friend of the very proper and very married Antony, Angelo relished his reputation as the country's sexiest bachelor—a title he'd twice been given by *San Rimini Today*. Given that publicity, together with Hollywood-worthy looks and his position in the upper echelons of San Rimini's national bank, Angelo always had the blonde waif of the moment by his side. And, unlike Antony and Marco, Angelo never seemed annoyed when women followed him along the Strada il Teatro trying to slip him their phone numbers. Or worse, their underwear. He reveled in the female attention, somehow managing it without looking like a womanizer.

Yet at this moment, the suave viscount seemed to have eyes only for the very intelligent, very brunette Amanda, a woman who'd never stuff her lingerie in a man's back pocket to capture his interest.

Marco glanced at his watch, checking how much time remained before he could announce that the guests should adjourn to the pier for the beginning of the race.

Damn. Still several minutes.

A wave of jealousy washed through him, and he fought to temper it. He had no claim on Amanda, didn't want any claim on her. In fact, it was best if she did find someone else to date while they were working together, even if that someone was Angelo Renati.

The viscount wasn't a bad guy. Just not the guy you'd pick for, say, your sister, given that he never stayed with any one woman very long. Still, if anyone could handle herself with Angelo, it was Amanda.

A friend of Federico's approached Marco to ask about the logistics of the boat race. Marco answered as best he could, telling himself he needed the distraction from Amanda. But when Angelo pointed out a yacht gliding past the palazzo, placing his hand on Amanda's shoulder when she turned to see, Marco politely excused himself, unable to keep from intruding on the pair.

"Angelo." He approached the window, certain his smile looked as fake as it felt. "I'm sorry we haven't had the chance to speak yet. How have you been?"

Viscount Renati dropped his hand from Amanda's shoulder and gave Marco a respectful nod. "Your Highness, a pleasure to see you." He spoke in fluent but accented English. "I was just telling Amanda how wonderful, and how out of character, it is for you to host such a stunning event. Quite a creative fundraiser you've conceived. I'm having a spectacular time, and I didn't even have to put on a suit."

Angelo winked at Amanda, and in a conspiratorial tone added, "His brother, Prince Antony, insists on hosting charity events that require formal attire. A relaxed party such as this better reflects Marco's personality."

"I'll take that as a compliment," Marco said. "Though I didn't plan it alone."

"I wondered about that." The viscount's Italian accent deepened a notch as he added, "Amanda tells me she has accepted a position at the palace."

Marco glanced at her. How much had Amanda revealed? In their two weeks of lessons, they'd never discussed how to handle questions about the nature of her employment. He hoped she understood that he didn't want it to become public knowledge. His personal reservations about his royal role needed to stay just that. Personal.

"That's correct. We're lucky to have her," he finally replied, trying to interpret Angelo's bemused expression. Remembering Amanda's advice about changing the topic of conversation, he directed a look at the clock on the far wall. "It's almost time for me to announce the beginning of the race."

"Amanda did not have the opportunity to explain the nature of her duties. Only that she is an employee at the palace."

Trepidation curled through Marco's gut as Angelo's gaze wandered over Amanda. The viscount smiled and he lifted a brow, though his eyes didn't leave Amanda. "What could you possibly have a beautiful American woman doing for you, Prince Marco? I am quite anxious to know."

Marco wracked his brain for a suitable answer, but he couldn't concentrate, not with Angelo eyeing Amanda as if she were a prized Chianti, ready to be sampled.

Luckily, Amanda seemed oblivious to the man's open perusal. She shrugged and said, "Now that the prince's military service has concluded, his focus has shifted to matters here in San Rimini. As is the case with his siblings, he will keep a staff to assist with the full range of his royal duties, including his charitable endeavors."

She handed her half-empty champagne flute to a tuxedoed waiter, then smiled at Angelo. "Thank you for taking the time to point out the sights, but I'm afraid duty calls. I'm sure we'll see each other outside."

Angelo opened his mouth as if he wanted to ask another question, but Amanda turned, effectively cutting off the viscount. Gesturing Marco toward the banquet hall's stage, she said, "Your Highness, you should urge your guests to move outdoors so you can explain the rules of today's race. I'll check with the palazzo staff to ensure everything is ready on the pier."

"Thank you," he said, careful to keep his tone formal in the hope that Angelo wouldn't pry further. Marco couldn't help but admire Amanda. She'd managed to respond to Angelo's question without giving away anything personal, and made him look the part of a responsible prince at the same time.

Amanda shook Viscount Renati's hand and said a quick, "It was a pleasure to meet you," but before she could walk off, he lifted her hand to his lips.

"I look forward to our next encounter."

Marco forced down another surge of jealousy as he envisioned the kisses he'd placed on that very hand in the rose garden.

Much as Marco liked Angelo, the man didn't deserve to kiss Amanda's hand. Not with the intention Marco suspected Angelo harbored.

"You're fishing in the wrong ocean this time," Marco chastised in a low voice once Amanda was out of earshot. "Amanda Hutton's not your type. Besides, I understand that you managed to catch Bianca Caratelli."

"Well, if you're going to get personal, Marco. For the moment, you're right. But that doesn't mean I can't continue to troll the waters for something better." The corners of the viscount's mouth curled. "Unless, of course, you're warning me off. You never did say why you hired her."

He'd stepped into that one. "I think she explained her role quite well."

"I don't know. Did she?"

Marco snorted. "Have I ever dated a staff member, Angelo?"

"As far as I know, you haven't employed a staff." The viscount's smile broadened. "Only one ancient assistant, whom I believe was hired by your father. Now, if you dated her, we need to have a talk about—"

"I have a staff now." Damn Angelo for being one of Antony's best friends and able to get away with personal jabs. And damn him for striking so close to the mark.

Marco turned his attention toward the stage, anxious to get away from Angelo before he asked any more questions. If the viscount suspected that Marco had feelings for Amanda beyond the professional, he wouldn't spread any rumors. He had too much honor, too much respect for the royal family. But if Angelo slipped and said something to Bianca Caratelli, his rumored girlfriend, she wouldn't show such restraint. It was well known throughout San Riminian society that the tabloids obtained a great deal of their inside information from her.

He gave Angelo a quick thump on the shoulder. "If you'll excuse me, I must direct my guests outside."

"Of course." The viscount adjusted a cuff on his gray shirt, one Marco knew had been made to order from an expensive Florentine shop, despite its relaxed style. "I am quite anxious to begin this afternoon's race. I have five entries."

Marco tried not to show his surprise as he thanked the viscount, knowing what he must have donated to have so many entries. "The Cancer Council will be grateful for your sponsorship. *Buona fortuna.*"

"And to you. I can't wait to see if your day is a success as well."

Marco summoned a confident smile, as if to say his success wasn't in doubt, but his mind silently answered Angelo, *you're not the only one.*

"QUITE A SUCCESS SO FAR," Amanda's voice came from behind him as he was about to address the crowd gathered along the pier for the start of the race. "Everyone seems to be enjoying themselves. And…"

Marco turned to see Amanda dangling a piece of paper in front of him.

"What's this?"

"The grand total. We just tallied the donations. You might want it for your introduction."

He took the page from her hand and did a double take when he saw the figure scrawled across it. "This much? You're certain?" At her nod, he said, "The Cancer Council will be thrilled."

Hell, *he* was thrilled. The thought that something he did, outside a night at the blackjack table, could pull in so much money for a good cause filled him with the unfamiliar sensation of a job well done. Then another thought occurred to him. "How many boats does that make?"

"Just over five hundred."

He must have looked as startled as he felt, because Amanda put a hand on his arm. Discreetly, but with enough pressure for reassurance. "The more boats, the more impressive it'll look, both to your guests and when posted to social media or on television."

He dragged his mind from the fact it was the first time she'd touched him since their first day in the library, when she'd put her hand over his on the desk and asked him to trust her.

He glanced at the water. "They won't clog the course?"

"I had the palazzo staff do a test run on Tuesday with seven hundred, just in case, and there were no problems. The sight will be memorable for everyone."

Marco tried not to look doubtful. Memorable could be good or bad.

Pushing the thought aside, he took the sheet of paper with him as he climbed atop a large pylon at the end of the pier. "Here goes."

"Hey, that's risky! You're supposed to stand at the end of the pier. Not balance on a post."

He shot her a look that said he had no intention of getting down.

"You'd better not fall off," Amanda whispered. Her professional smile remained in place, but her eyes displayed her worry over his choice to stand in such a precarious position.

"Now that would be memorable," he told her as the crowd noticed him and began to quiet. For a brief moment, he thought falling off might be preferable to speaking in front of such a large crowd.

Instead, he barreled on, holding the sheet of paper in the air and raising his voice so the group assembled on the pier could hear him. "I've been handed a very important note. Now that all the entries are in, I can confirm that—thanks to all of you—today's event has doubled our fundraising goal for the San Riminian Cancer Council."

At his words, the crowd clapped furiously, and a few whistles could be heard. When it quieted again, he spoke for a few minutes about the Council, its mission and its past successes, and finished by reminding them of all that was raised through the event. "As you might guess, such a large sum will go a long way toward funding cancer research. I thank all of you for coming and for giving so generously. I am proud to count you among my friends."

It was a bit of a stretch. They weren't friends so much as members of the circle he'd been compelled to socialize with since birth. But as they continued to cheer him on, he realized that as much as he hated crowds, and as much as he despised public speaking, seeing his countrymen open their hearts and their wallets to help others gave him a sense of satisfaction.

In that moment, he understood, at least a little, why his siblings so enjoyed their public role.

He allowed that positive feeling to drive him as he turned the guests' attention to the upcoming race.

"Of course, you realize that in addition to helping the San Riminian Cancer Council, your generosity has entitled each of you to" —he reached down to grab the small white rubber object Amanda had ready for him, then held it aloft— "a racing craft of the highest caliber!"

Where had that come from? He'd memorized precisely what he was going to say, and that wasn't it.

Laughter echoed across the pier. Not false, laughing-to-be-polite laughter. Sincere, hearty laughter. He glanced at Amanda, whose expression was somewhere between upbeat and I-told-you-so.

The metal rod he'd imagined running up his spine during the cocktail hour disappeared as he took in the genuine smiles of his guests and breathed in the fresh air of the Adriatic. Adrenaline pumped through his body, almost as if he were involved in a full-throttle, competitive boat race out on the open waves.

Perhaps he could have fun with this. Be himself and see what happened, just as Amanda had urged him to do several times during their role playing.

He continued, "Several hundred of these impressive feats of marine engineering—"

Another round of laughs.

"—are in the large boxes located beside me, at the end of the pier. When you made your donation, you each received a ticket entitling you to the rubber duck—that is, rubber boat—of your choice. Take your time to choose carefully, for your goal is to select the boat you feel has the best chance of winning."

"Any tips for novice racers?" a voice called out from the crowd. It sounded like Angelo, but he couldn't be sure.

He smiled and flipped the boat in his palm to display its hull. "Well, you might note the fine lines of this small but sturdy craft" —he squinted at the tiny lettering— "made in Taiwan of only the finest rubber. You're looking for something that will move smoothly along the course, as you would if you were selecting a craft for the Bellonini brothers," he said, referring to the country's most famous speedboat racers.

As the people gathered below him looked toward the boxes, he noticed that many of them held more than one ticket in their hands. Clearly, they were as devoted to the cause of battling cancer as he was. He cleared his throat and added, "If your donation today was made in honor of someone close to you, I encourage you to write that person's name on the side of your boat. Markers are available beside the boxes. Perhaps, in years to come, there will be fewer people in the world faced with a cancer diagnosis, and those who are will have a much better prognosis."

A round of cheers, this time filled with emotion, rose from the crowd.

"One final thing," he pointed to the bottom of his boat, "and this is important. On whichever craft you choose, you should note the bar code on the bottom. This is your craft's entry number. Before you place your boat in the water," he indicated a large bin at the start of the racecourse, just behind him, "be sure to record your name and entry number on the log. No name and number in the log, no prize."

A low rumble of oooohs met his statement.

"As you know," he continued, "the grand prize is a week at my family's private cabin in Tyrol at the height of the ski season, complete with a private chef, housekeeping service, and access to rental equipment should you need it." Applause broke out on the pier. He hadn't been sure he could convince his father to give up the cabin to someone outside the royal family for a week, as it had never been done before. However, Marco knew such an extraordinary prize would draw a large number of entries, and his father had never been one to turn down an opportunity to help the San Riminian Cancer Council.

Marco added, "Now, since you know I'm the last person in San Rimini to lecture others about rules," a wave of knowing comments floated through the crowd, "let's get to it. Select your boats, log your number and place them at the start, and we're off!"

With whoops and cheers, the guests turned en masse toward the boxes of boats. Marco finally allowed himself to exhale. The worst part of the day, or at least the part he feared would be worst, was over. And without a single misstep.

As he turned away from the crowd to jump off the post, two guests brushed by him on their way to select their boats. He barely felt the impact on his hip, but it was enough to cause his foot to catch the rough edge. He swiveled, overcompensated, and the blue waves and the weathered wood of the pier tilted before him as instinct forced him to circle his arms in a desperate struggle to regain his balance.

No, this can't be happening.

He was about to ruin the whole afternoon by plunging headfirst into San Rimini Bay.

CHAPTER 7

"MARCO!" Amanda watched in dismay as two guests bumped into the prince at the exact moment he took his foot off the wooden post to jump down. On instinct, she reached for his arm, latching onto his wrist just as he managed to regain his balance enough to leap toward the pier instead of making an embarrassing splashdown.

The slats vibrated near her feet as he hit, but he straightened quickly, making his near-disaster appear intentional. Amanda heaved a sigh of relief and let go.

"Surprise, surprise. You finally called me Marco." He quirked an eyebrow at her and smoothed his polo shirt, mock innocence on his face. "Is something wrong, Ms. Hutton?"

"My mistake, and you know what's wrong," she hissed, but couldn't resist adding, "I specifically told you not to fall."

"Who said I fell?" He glanced around the pier, making a show of the fact that none of the guests, who were now engaged in debating the merits of various rubber boats, had appeared to notice his misstep. "Besides, every so often you have to take some risks. It was easier to get everyone's attention from up there. Don't you ever take risks?"

"Never. I knew balancing up there would be trouble." Her tone was reprimanding, but she allowed humor to seep into her expression. "You got lucky, Your Highness."

"Well, then," he put a hand on her shoulder in a manner that felt entirely too personal, and entirely too good. "Maybe that luck will carry over to the race."

She tried to ignore the way his hand warmed her skin, even through the fabric of her navy dress. "So long as you don't jump into the water, everything will fine. You've handled the most challenging part, between the cocktail hour and the introduction."

"That's not what I meant. I was talking about the race itself. And winning it."

Her brows lifted in question. "You couldn't enter."

"No, but you're not connected to the race in any official capacity, so nothing's stopping you. I put two entries in your name." He reached down to the base of the pylon and picked up a small brown box she hadn't noticed before. He lifted the lid to reveal two rubber boats identical to those in the large boxes the guests now rifled through.

She opened her mouth to protest, but he quieted her with a shake of his head. "Hey, after putting up with me these last two weeks, you deserve a vacation at a luxury cabin. Even if you're not the winner, I knew you'd want to show your support to the Cancer Council. These two entries were made in honor of your mother and your aunt."

A lump of emotion filled her throat as she took the two boats from the box. One had her mother's name written on the side, the other was inscribed with her aunt's name. How could he have known? Then she met his gaze and realized. "Your father told you."

He nodded. His placed his hand on her shoulder once more as he explained, "Not to invade your privacy, though. When I left the library after our third or fourth session, I ran into my father. He wanted to know how our arrangement was working. I told him I wasn't sure, and that's when he told me. He wanted me to know that you might understand me—and what I went through adjusting to palace life after my mother passed away—more than I believed." Marco shrugged. "He was right. Given that the fundraiser is for the Cancer Council, well, it seemed an appropriate way to thank you."

Everything in her wanted to kiss him, to wrap her hand around the back of his neck and pull his face to hers. To make up for leaving him in the garden the night of the wedding, when she'd sensed he needed her. And to thank him for being so sweet, even though the last thing Marco diTalora would want to be thought of was sweet.

She swallowed hard. Given the presence of the paparazzi on the shore and the fact that the guests would start paying attention to him again any minute, there would be no kissing. It felt dangerous even thinking about it.

He must have sensed her heightened emotions, because he dropped his hand from her shoulder and quickly added, "I think that's why my father hired you, instead of having some stuffed shirt lecture me on the proper form of address for cabinet ministers. He figured you'd understand me and the way I think. And there's your wealth of experience tutoring adults, of course."

That broke the spell, and she laughed. The idea of Marco locked in a room listening to a staid lecture on the proper forms of address was ludicrous. "Now you're trying to flatter me. Don't think this will get you out of more lessons."

"Who, me? I'd never butter up the teacher." He tilted his head toward the guests. "This afternoon hasn't been perfect. I still feel awkward with everyone looking at me, studying my every move. And I needed you to bail me out when Angelo—Viscount Renati—started asking all those questions. But it's going better than I hoped. I'm actually having fun. And you deserve the thanks."

Amanda prayed her cheeks didn't look as flushed as they felt. "The entries weren't necessary. I was just doing my job." But their arrangement made it more than a mere job, and they both knew it. She met his gaze, but found it unreadable. "This was very kind of you. Thank you."

"I hope one's a winner. Then I'll give you the cabin tour myself."

Whether he was blatantly flirting or making a matter-of-fact statement, Amanda couldn't tell, and she sure wasn't going to ask. As much as her heart wished for flirting, her brain told her it would be stupid, stupid, stupid. For one, Prince Marco *flirted*, he didn't have relationships. Intimacy wasn't part of his emotional makeup. According to Jennifer, he even seemed content with the idea of an arranged marriage. On the other hand, she dreamed of a relationship, one like Jennifer and Antony's. Or like King Eduardo and Queen Aletta's must have been.

And for two, even if she decided she could handle flirting-without-strings-attached, the outcome Marco probably expected was one that would get her fired.

She smiled as if he'd said nothing out of the ordinary, then made her way across the pier to give her entry numbers to Harriet Hunt, Prince Antony's assistant, who'd volunteered to help with the fundraiser while Antony and Jennifer were away on their honeymoon.

Turning from Harriet, Amanda carried her two white boats to the nearly full, large metal bin that hung off the side of the pier and over the red buoy-enclosed racecourse. She squeezed each boat, thought of how fortunate she was that her aunt and mother were alive, then tossed them on top.

A few other guests came up behind her to add their boats to the bin as Marco called for the log and ceremoniously snapped it shut.

He whistled for quiet, then strode to the bin and put a hand on a smooth lever protruding from the side. He called out, "The race is simple. The boats will drop from this bin to the sea. The red markers will keep them from drifting off course, and the tide will push them the length of the pier, back to the shore. First boat to ground itself on the sand wins. In the event of a tie, both entrants will win a week at the cabin. If everyone's ready? On your mark..."

"Get set!" the crowd joined in.

"Go!"

With that, he pushed the lever, opening a hatch on the bottom of the bin. From the corner of her eye, Amanda caught the flash of the paparazzi's cameras as the white boats plunged into the water. The waves and the wind quickly pushed them along the racecourse toward the beach, about the distance of two soccer fields.

Cheers rose from the crowd as they made their way along the pier, following the white wave back toward the Palazzo d'Avorio and the finish line. Occasionally a whoop or whistle could be heard, though no one could possibly identify their own entry among the hundreds bobbing in unison.

As Amanda and Marco had discussed while planning the event, the prince gradually zigzagged his way to the front of the crowd, shaking hands and chatting with guests as he went. By the time the group reached the shore, he'd taken the lead. Amanda forced herself not to stare as he sat on the side of the pier at the spot it met the beach, then slid off his shoes and socks with more grace than she thought possible for a man of his build. He rolled up his khaki pants and hopped down to the sand so he could pluck the winning boat from its resting place. Despite his beachcomber look, Marco still displayed an assured, regal air. No one could possibly suspect his inner discomfort at hosting the event. He'd captivated every person in the crowd, including her.

The boats bobbed toward the shore just as Marco's bare feet met the tide. Finally, when a wave receded, a lone boat remained beached a few steps in front of the prince. He reached down, flipped it over, then called out, "Number one-six two!"

Harriet Hunt repeated, "Entry number one-six-two," then announced, "The Honorable Bernardo Raffini!"

The gray-haired judge stepped forward with his hands clasped over his head in victory. The perfect winner, Amanda decided as she applauded. She'd talked to the judge briefly during the cocktail hour, and he'd mentioned that he was planning to retire in a few months. A week at a mountaintop hideaway in the beautiful Tyrolean Alps would be the perfect reward for a long career in service to his country.

Not that she wouldn't have appreciated the vacation herself, especially if Marco had followed through on his promise to give her a private tour.

She smoothed her hands over the front of her dress, as if doing so would brush away the thought, then focused her attention on the judge, who accepted a set of symbolic keys to the retreat from the prince. She clapped along with the rest of the crowd.

Whatever made her so obsessed with Marco diTalora? She'd met good-looking men before, wealthy men, connected men. Men whose bodies were honed with muscle and hard planes in all the right places to give a woman incredible dreams. Yet those men hadn't affected her quite the way Marco had. She was hired to instruct him, for crying out loud, not moon over him. What was wrong with her?

But as the guests wandered inside and she and Harriet started gathering the rest of the boats as they drifted ashore, at least two of which were in honor of her aunt and mother, she knew.

Prince Marco diTalora had trusted her. And in doing so, he had shown her his heart.

AMANDA TAPPED her pen against the ruled notepad sitting before her on the library desktop. She'd spent the last few minutes scribbling down a list of areas she and Marco needed to work on, as well as a list of things to follow up on the Cancer Council event.

After the race, she'd encouraged the prince to mingle with his guests. At the event's conclusion, she'd taken her leave, telling Marco to enjoy a well-deserved night off and spend it with his friends. They'd agreed to meet in the library this morning after breakfast.

She had the impression he was about to invite her to join him and his friends, but she'd managed to avoid giving him the opportunity. She'd desperately needed to tear herself from his presence to settle her thoughts, not to mention her hormones. After a long, cool shower and a night spent considering her duties, she'd awakened ready to work.

Marco entered the library with a cup of coffee in each hand and a lazy smile on his face. Though she suspected he'd been out until the wee hours of the morning, he didn't look it. His hair was ruffled, as always, but he'd shaved, his gray slacks skimmed his hips without a wrinkle in sight, and he wore a pressed black shirt left slightly open at the collar. The overall effect was relaxed, but pulled together. "Ready to caffeinate?"

"I've already caffeinated, but I could use more." Grateful, she gestured to the coasters at the desktop's edge. When he set down the cups, she saw his was black, but hers contained the exact amount of milk she always added.

"I saw Samuel Barden in the breakfast room," he explained, referring to the chef in charge of serving the family. "He said this is how you take it."

She was touched Marco had thought to ask. "Thank you."

He leaned his perfect body across the desk and wrinkled his forehead as he pretended to study her list. "That bad, huh? I thought I did extraordinarily well."

"You did. In fact, I was thrilled with the way it turned out." Amanda dropped the pen onto the desktop and stood, stretching her legs. "But there's always room for improvement. Your father expects you to attend more functions than the occasional charity event. An offhand joke or two about rubber boats will only carry you so far. You'll need to sharpen both your conversational and presentation skills so you'll be prepared."

"For what? Has he told you what he has planned?"

"No, but I can guess. There will be meetings with local officials, various government ceremonies, state dinners—"

A look of alarm crossed his face. "A state dinner? Not soon, I hope."

"No, not soon. But you'll be expected to attend as many social occasions as possible. Your assistant tells me there are at least thirty invitations on her desk now that it's known you're back home to stay. And I read in yesterday's paper that the National Public Library is nearly finished with their renovations. They've sent a request for a member of the royal family to speak at the reopening. It would be the perfect opportunity for you."

"Sounds like a lot."

"It is," she admitted. "Like it or not, being a prince is a full-time job."

"I suppose." He straightened, apparently unwilling to think about it.

"Don't worry. It'll become second nature soon enough. The more practice you have, the easier it will become. Meeting with a foreign head of state won't seem any more difficult than hosting the boat race. I'll make sure of it."

His eyes crinkled as he smiled. "I bet you will."

She tore her page of notes from the pad and rose. "First things first, however. This morning, I'd like you to draft a note of thanks to those who attended yesterday's event. Say something about the importance of their participation, give an example of how the San Riminian Cancer Council will use their donation, et cetera. And put a personal note in Judge Raffini's letter to congratulate him on his win. Tell him you think it'll be a nice way to start his retirement, though you're sorry to lose him as an active member of the judiciary."

He grabbed a blank piece of paper from the notepad, then jotted down *thank yous* and *Judge Raffini* as reminders. "You're good at this, you know?"

"I know." She resisted the urge to punctuate the statement with a self-satisfied smile.

"About Judge Raffini." He set down his pen and met her eyes, his gaze suddenly serious. "I'm sorry you didn't win. I know I'm supposed to be impartial, but I was rooting for you. You deserved that prize more than anyone else there."

She felt herself blush. Again. It unnerved her that her cheeks burned whenever he opened his mouth around her. "I appreciate that, and the thought that went into your donation, but it wouldn't have been appropriate if I'd won. Far better for a guest to walk away with the prize than someone connected to organizing the event."

He moved around the desk to stand beside her, so close she realized his hair still held dampness from his morning shower. She could smell whatever soap he'd used as heat rose from his skin. The combination struck her as masculine, warm, and unforgivably attractive. She sidestepped, intending to walk around the desk to put some distance between them.

"I have to admit, I had purely selfish reasons, as well." He shifted to block her path. "I was hoping to show you my family's winter lodge. I spent some wonderful days there when I was young, sledding with my sister and brothers, and skiing with my parents. Anyway, I think you'd have enjoyed it."

"It's not as if you couldn't show me another time," she pointed out, then instantly regretted the words. She'd just invited herself to spend time with him—time alone—in a secluded cabin, which was wrong on two fronts. One didn't flirt with a prince, nor invite oneself to a royal residence. At the moment, she wasn't sure which was the greater fault.

But it didn't matter. The attraction between them was palpable.

"Of course," she quickly added, "given how well the event went yesterday, I doubt your father will keep past my three-month term of employment. I'll be back in the States before ski season, so it wouldn't have made sense for me to win a week at the lodge anyway."

He moved a step closer, leaning in enough for her to feel his warm breath against her face. "Too bad," he replied, his voice soft near her ear. "Yesterday was fun. I can only imagine what a ski trip with you might be like."

Her resolve wavered. If she wanted to, she could reach for his shoulder, then slide a hand around to the back of his neck. Wait and see how he'd react.

No, deep down, she knew how he'd react. And she knew how much she wanted it.

Instead, she turned toward the desk, giving herself a margin of safety, and cleared her throat. "I'm sure Judge Raffini and his family will enjoy it."

"They don't ski," he murmured, turning his back to the desk, then reaching to tuck a strand of hair behind her ear. His light touch electrified her, and she moved away, needing to escape, but found herself pinned between the desk and the library wall. His hands went to the wall on either side of her. "At least, his wife doesn't."

"Neither do I."

"Ah. So you aren't an expert at everything."

"I never claimed to be." Her voice came out in a breathless rasp, even to her own ears.

His gaze roamed over her face with tantalizing slowness. As much as instinct warned her to duck under his arm, to get to the other side of the room and away from his intimate perusal, she couldn't. His gaze held more than desire; there was caring there, too.

"Tell me, Amanda," his voice came out low and smooth, and she loved the way her name rolled off his tongue. "What's your professional opinion on a student giving his teacher a more personal thank you for a job well done?"

CHAPTER 8

"You already thanked me. You brought me coffee. And the two boats…doing that meant a lot."

"What you did meant a lot. You found an event that suited *me*. Not my father, not the press, not the palace buzzards." His mouth was a whisper away from hers. He tucked another loose strand of hair behind her ear, then moved his head to drop an easy, gentle kiss where the hair had been on her cheek. "You treat me with respect, but don't take my crap, either. That means the most of all, because no one has treated me that way before. No one has seen me the way you see me."

For two weeks, they'd kept their relationship professional. But yesterday's shared success and the personal nature of his gift changed things, and they both knew it. They'd both *felt* it, long before he brought her coffee or moved to trap her between his body and the library wall. The intimacy brought on by yesterday's event brought them both right back to their heated moment in the rose garden.

It was why she'd refused to join him the night before. He'd allowed her the distance then. He was forcing her to confront the issue now.

"How is it that you have no trouble talking to me in the most, the most" —she fought for the right word— "forthright manner, but hate to speak to a room full of people?"

"Because I'd never say these words to a room full of people."

"You shouldn't say them to me, either." Her eyes met his, and she saw her own emotions mirrored there. Before she could think, her hands went to his waist. "I could—"

The words *get fired* never came out. His lips brushed over hers, as tender and full of promise as they'd been on her wrist two weeks earlier.

All sense of logic left her as he kissed her again. This time, however, the action was decisive. Possessive. She opened to him, meeting his kiss, pulling him closer. Her hands skidded around his hips, and a shudder rolled through her as her palms met the strong, solid muscles of his back. He cupped her chin, melding her mouth to his.

Marco diTalora had to be the perfect male.

The exhale that escaped her worked like a pressure valve, suddenly permitting the release of two weeks of pent-up longing. He pressed her against the library wall, tenderness vanishing as his body fit perfectly to hers. The chair rail bit into her rear, but she didn't care. She fought to draw him even closer, digging her fingers into his shirt, wrapping one leg around the back of his calf. As Marco's mouth savaged hers, one of his hands slid lower, to her shoulder, and then to her hip, to untuck her blouse. He moved as if possessed, with little care for the possibility of torn fabric or lost buttons.

As the heat of his palm singed the bare skin of her lower back, she suddenly knew what it would be like to share a bed with him. Pure, sweet heaven.

And she wanted it.

She wanted nights of wild, athletic sex in every corner of his private apartment or the ski lodge, followed by soft, gentle kisses each morning over breakfast. Then more lovemaking, each time more daring, more adventurous.

She reached for his face, her body's appetite for him turning ravenous, even as her mind screamed for her to stop.

His head dipped lower, his tongue teasing the hollow of her neck. A soft moan escaped her at the sensation, and she opened her eyes to see her fingers woven into his sun-bleached hair. His head was moving lower, his mouth now at the edge of her bra, slowly moving it aside. At some point, he'd undone the top buttons of her blouse.

Prim, *proper* Amanda Hutton should never be doing this. With sudden clarity, she realized the library door stood wide open.

"Marco," she breathed, "Please, we can't—"

"We can." His voice came to her muffled, his lips not even leaving her skin as he spoke.

"But we shouldn't." She closed her eyes and allowed her hands to fall from where she'd entangled them. Even if they weren't caught, even if he somehow decided he wanted more than flirting from her, she could never have the relationship with Marco that she desired.

What she carried inside could devastate him.

He finally tore himself away and met her eyes, his face a mix of bare need and frustration. He studied her for a moment as if gauging how serious she could be, given the fact her blouse was now open far enough to display the top of her pink lace bra to anyone who might happen to walk by the library.

"You're right." His expression turned blank, then he started to button her blouse with as much dexterity as he'd unbuttoned it.

"I'm sorry," she whispered.

"Don't be. You have nothing to apologize for." He finished buttoning her blouse, then framed her face in his hands. "You're a fascinating, gorgeous woman. We've been cooped up in this library for weeks now, and we got carried away in a moment of success. It was amazing, but if you say so, it won't happen again."

She couldn't speak. She could only stare at him. She wanted him, and he knew it.

He studied her for a moment, then released her and spun on his heel. Grabbing his notes from the desk, he said, "I'll get to work on the thank you letters. When I'm finished, we can start on the rest of your list."

"Your Highness—"

"It's Marco! My name is Marco."

He strode out the library door, leaving Amanda leaning against the library wall in a daze.

———————

HE SHOULDN'T HAVE DONE it.

With any other woman, fine. But with Amanda Hutton? The woman practically had the words Seeking Long Term Relationship emblazoned on her forehead. All he wanted was a little flirting, maybe a quick tumble.

Didn't he?

He stalked down the hallway, putting as much distance as he could between himself and Amanda.

She was beyond beautiful. And brilliant. No doubt about that. But as a young, eligible prince, he was introduced to women with both beauty and brains every day. So what was it about her that made him burn with jealousy when Angelo openly admired her? Why did his mouth go dry the moment he'd entered the library and saw her scribbling away? And why couldn't he have kept his hands to himself? He'd reached to fix her hair, and the feel of that stray strand curled in his fingers intoxicated him beyond the point of caring about propriety, or being discovered by anyone on the staff who happened by the library.

It was idiocy.

He swallowed hard as he rounded a corner. He had to control himself. He'd only end up costing Amanda her job and, unbelievable as it would have been only a couple of weeks ago, he found himself looking forward to their lessons.

Besides, even if he didn't get her fired, she'd certainly be hurt when his father started making noise about arranging his marriage to someone with wealth and a pedigree. With both Federico and Antony married, and his father's heart surgery behind him, it might not be long before the king turned his attention toward Marco's future beyond attending palace functions.

It was the last thing he wanted.

He ran a hand over his jaw. He could still feel Amanda's touch at his waist, and the soft slip of her mouth beneath his. He burned for her. At the same time, she had a gift for making him comfortable in his own skin, and that talent went beyond mastering the art of diplomacy. It was a dangerous combination, one that could make him reliant, and the last thing on earth he wanted was to rely on another human being. He didn't need the pain it inevitably caused when they left. Or—he thought as he passed under a painting that depicted his father on the throne with Queen Aletta at his side—when they died.

He took a long breath, then blew it out slowly. The day of his mother's funeral service had started out with overcast skies. He'd walked to the Duomo behind the 1750 State Coach—its interior empty for the procession, as was tradition to honor a lost king or queen—in a fog that matched the weather. But after the service, he'd emerged from the cathedral to sunny skies and thousands upon thousands of faces. In that moment, a gaping hole had opened in his chest. Given the weather and the number of people holding flags, it appeared more like a parade crowd than a funeral crowd, despite the expressions of mourning, and it gnawed at him.

The citizens of San Rimini had lost an icon. He'd lost his anchor. He'd sworn never again to be so adrift.

He slammed his hand on the leg of a marble statue as he reached the foot of the stairs that would take him to his private residence. "Damn!"

"Marco!"

Marco stopped short. Where had the voice come from?

The king approached from a side door. He didn't bother to hide the displeasure from his face. "Marco, do not curse. I won't have it, especially in the hall. Your voice carries and anyone on the staff could hear you."

Marco fought the urge to roll his eyes. Instead, he gestured to the sheaf of papers his father carried. "What are those?"

"Notes on past economic agreements."

"For your meeting with the Greek minister?"

King Eduardo nodded. "He arrived this morning. We meet in

about an hour, then he will address parliament. Representatives from several of the Balkan nations arrive this afternoon. We have a plan that will improve trade for our entire region." He shifted the stack of papers to his other arm, then considered his youngest son. "And tonight, you shall be hosting them all for dinner."

This time, Marco did roll his eyes. "Very funny."

"This isn't a joke."

The lines between the king's eyes deepened, and Marco realized his father was indeed serious.

"Are you trying to derail the plan before it's complete?" he asked. "I have zero experience hosting an evening like that. At best, I can attend as a guest and make small talk. Besides, I thought Federico was hosting the dinner. Half of parliament will be there. Not to mention—"

"I am familiar with the guest list," the king interrupted him. "And I would host it if I could. But you know that the Queen Aletta wing of Royal Memorial Hospital is being dedicated tonight. It's been planned for nearly two years and I absolutely must attend. The ministers knew that when we scheduled our talks for this week. I'd planned for Federico to handle tonight's dinner, but Lucrezia is ill and he needs to be with her."

"What's wrong?" Marco couldn't imagine the duty-bound Federico missing a state function. He wasn't sure Federico had *ever* missed such an event, even for his wife. In fact, she'd insist he attend.

"She has a headache. Not her usual migraine, apparently. I don't know any more than that."

"What about Isabella?"

"She's in Venice overnight. She's going to be the master of ceremonies at the film festival next year, and there's a preliminary meeting—"

"Get her back." A wave of nausea swept through him, and he fought to contain his growing panic. "I can't possibly host a dinner of that importance, let alone in less than twelve hours. I was fortunate to get through yesterday's fundraiser. If Amanda hasn't given you her report yet—"

"Come with me."

Without allowing Marco room for argument, the king strode past him. Marco groaned and followed his father down the hall, knowing the king wouldn't be dissuaded. When his father made an abrupt turn into the library, the prince wasn't the least bit surprised.

He hoped Amanda didn't look as flustered as she had a moment before, when he'd done his kiss-and-run routine.

And he hoped to hell she'd tucked in her blouse.

CHAPTER 9

Amanda stared at the desktop, trying to concentrate on the lists she'd started before Marco kissed her—if one could term what had passed between them only a kiss—but the words wouldn't come into focus.

She'd accepted this job knowing she found him attractive, and she'd promised herself she wouldn't get involved. The professional price was too high, let alone the personal price.

How could she be so stupid?

Then there was the bigger question: What had prompted Prince Marco's sudden walkout? It had to be more than her simple protest of *we shouldn't*. He'd wanted her as much as she'd wanted him, and been more than willing to continue despite their relatively public location. All it would have taken was a few steps across the room to close the door. Anyone who walked by would assume they were role-playing conversations, as they'd done many times over the previous two weeks. But when Marco had lifted his head and met her gaze, something in him froze. She could almost see his mind change.

Perhaps her expression had given her away. Perhaps he'd seen that in those few, stolen moments, she'd allowed herself to imagine what it would be like to awaken beside him on a regular basis, to share not only a bed but a future with him.

She balled her hands into fists in her lap. She'd known Marco diTalora's reputation before they'd met. And she'd understood his reluctance to give his heart to a woman the minute she'd realized how much his mother's death had affected him. Hadn't Jennifer mentioned at the wedding that Marco didn't object to an arranged marriage? From what she knew of such marriages, they were primarily made to forge alliances, strengthen political ties. For practical purposes. Not for love, at least not at first. If there was love, it came later.

For her to lose control of her emotions with a man like Marco, to kiss him the way she had—she flexed her fingers in anger—she'd given away far too much, and it left her with a sick feeling in the pit of her stomach.

"Ms. Hutton."

Her head snapped up at the regal tone. Shoving her notepad aside, she scrambled to her feet. "Your Highness, I'm surprised to see you here. If I'd known—"

King Eduardo raised a hand, urging her to relax. "It's all right, Ms. Hutton. Have a seat."

She eased into the desk chair as Marco entered the room behind his father. Her face heated at the sight of him, so she kept her attention on the king.

"You're aware that there is a dinner scheduled for tonight here in the palace?" At her nod, he continued, "I have discussed the event with Prince Marco, and I would like him to attend."

"He wants me to *host* it," Marco clarified.

Amanda looked from Marco to the king. "I didn't realize you needed him prepared for such an occasion so soon, Your Highness. He only hosted his first event yesterday, and that was outdoors, in a more relaxed setting."

"Yes," Eduardo came forward, setting a stack of papers on the desk in front of her. "One of my good friends, Count Giovanni Sozzani, was in attendance. He was quite impressed. I see that I hired the right person for the task."

Amanda wondered what the king would have to say if he knew the right person for the task had been groping his son with her blouse wide open in that very room only minutes before.

"I appreciate the kind words, but I'm not sure the success of yesterday's event means that Prince Marco is ready to host a formal dinner." She hesitated, not wanting to contradict the king. "Given the importance of your economic plan, you need the evening to go off without a hitch. Might I suggest Prince Federico or Princess Isabella handle the task? Though I'm happy for Prince Marco to have the opportunity to attend, of course. It will be a good learning experience."

"I'm sure it will be," the king conceded. He looked to Marco, who remained standing against the far wall of the library. Something about the prince's posture gave Amanda a sense of unease.

"They can't do it, can they?"

"I'm afraid not," the monarch replied. "Federico planned to serve as host, but his wife is ill." The king's gaze bored into Amanda, assessing her. "I apologize for the lack of time to prepare."

She swallowed hard. "We'll manage, Your Highness. I hope Lucrezia recovers quickly."

King Eduardo tapped the pile of papers. "Prince Marco will need to be familiar with this by tonight, so he can speak with some knowledge about the plan. There's no need to lobby the various dignitaries, or for Marco to have more than a rough grasp of the issues involved. They know he was not involved in drafting the plan. I just want everyone kept happy until tomorrow. Am I understood?" He looked from Amanda to Marco.

"Understood," the two replied in unison, though Marco sounded far from confident.

"Ms. Hutton, I shall have a selection of appropriate gowns, shoes, and handbags sent to your room so that you may attend the dinner as well. I expect that's all you need?"

She nodded, trying to comprehend how much work she had to do in a very short period of time.

"Good. I meet with the Greek minister shortly, then will accompany him to parliament. If you need anything, contact my assistant. She can answer any questions you might have."

He turned for the door, but looked back at her before stepping into the hall. "I expect tonight to be a success, Ms. Hutton."

"Yes, Your Highness."

He tipped his head in acknowledgment, then departed, pulling the door closed behind him.

Marco stared at her for a long, breathless moment.

"Well, I suppose those thank you notes are on hold," she ventured. The joke fell flat.

"Listen—"

She held up a hand. "Let's not talk about it, okay? We're pressed for time as it is." She couldn't bear to discuss what had passed between them, anyway. All he'd do was break her heart, and that was the last thing she needed with the pressure of tonight's dinner weighing on her shoulders.

A flash of emotion—relief? regret?—glimmered in his clear blue eyes, then disappeared. "Fine."

She tore her gaze from his and gestured to the stack of paper. "This is no big deal, really."

"Looks like a big deal to me."

"This is just background. Like reading the newspaper so you'll know what happened in the world the previous day. You skim it, absorb what you can. You don't have to memorize it all."

His mouth twitched in doubt.

"You heard your father. All you have to do tonight is keep the dignitaries happy. You don't even have to talk to them one on one about economic matters, if that makes you uncomfortable. Ask about their spouses, tell them what you admire about their countries, that sort of thing. If you find common ground—a vacation they've taken that you're curious about, a movie you both enjoyed—you'll be fine. After yesterday, you've proven you can handle that."

"Then why all the economic updates?"

She worried her lip. He wasn't going to like what she had to say. "You'll be expected to say something at dinner. These dignitaries are in San Rimini for a reason. A few words are called for about the importance of maintaining strong economies and relationships throughout the region."

"I don't think—"

"You won't have to say much. You won't even need to speak for the length of time you did at the race yesterday. We'll write it out beforehand, and we'll get in a few practice runs."

He approached the desk and swept up the papers. "I should start on this. Perhaps I should go to my apartment." His attention slipped past her to the wall behind the desk, apparently noticing what she had after he'd left. A few books had tipped over on the adjacent shelf, likely when he'd had her up against the wall.

Amanda forced herself not to turn around and look. She'd taken a seat to try to clear her brain without pausing to right the books first.

"Yes, I think that's best," she told him. "In the meantime, I'll draft something general for you to say. While you're reading, you'll likely come across a few details worth adding. Can you be back in an hour?"

"Let's make it ninety minutes. There's a lot here."

She nodded. As he moved to go, she added, "Prince Marco? One last thing."

He paused, and she puffed out a breath. "While these politicians know you had nothing to do with negotiating these new policies, they believe you have your father's ear. If they believe any issues are unresolved, they'll ply you with their opinions, hoping you'll persuade your father to see things their way. Maybe even convince him to amend things slightly in their favor."

Marco pulled a face. "That can't happen."

"But they don't know that, and it's good for your public image for them to believe you have more power than you do. Like letting an opponent think you have a better poker hand than you really hold. So go ahead and listen to what they have to say. Tell them their point of view is interesting or something to think about, but go no further. Don't tell them it's good or bad, don't take a stance. And whatever you do, don't let yourself be intimidated. You're a diTalora, and they're on your turf."

Marco's sharp gaze met hers, and Amanda was relieved to see the hint of a smile there.

"Point noted. But don't you be intimidated by the state dining room. This might be a pretty nice setup," he twirled a finger to indicate the library, with its now-familiar curtains and antique rugs, "but the state dining room blows it away. It's a whole different kind of elegant. When you see it, you'll understand why I'm concerned about pulling this off."

She gave him a look of confidence as he moved toward the library door. "Be back in ninety minutes to practice your speech."

———

Marco might not be able to pull this off.

Even with years of formal events—and now one royal wedding— under her belt, Amanda had to force herself not to gape as she reached the top of the marble staircase and entered the reception hall outside the royal palace's state dining room.

She brushed her hand against her beaded black gown, thankful the king had sent it to her room. It fit her perfectly: a waist that nipped in without being tight, spaghetti straps cut to the proper length, and fabric that slipped over her skin, making it lightweight despite the beading. Though understated, its fine construction meant it had likely cost a fortune. Nothing Amanda owned would have been worthy of such an elegant setting. While she'd seen the reception hall and state dining room once before, on a PBS special featuring the world's most elegant palaces, it didn't compare to viewing the rooms in person.

The hall itself wasn't really a hall. Rather, the room was perfectly round. Beneath Amanda's feet, the polished hardwood floor boasted a sun-shaped inlay consisting of at least seven different types of wood. The rays of the sun shot out in all directions, emphasizing the room's unusual shape. In front of her, double doors opening to the state dining room curved to fit into the wall. On either side of the doors, windows trimmed in gilt offered impressive views of the glittering city, with its posh restaurants, casinos, theaters, and hotels. Overhead, a chandelier boasting thousands of teardrop-shaped crystals bathed the room in light.

Even more impressive than the reception hall's decor were the people who now occupied it. While Jennifer and Antony's wedding included several representatives from Europe's royal families, tonight's dinner boasted a political guest list that rivaled any party her father had attended during his days as ambassador to Italy.

Leaders of several Balkan nations gathered near one window, sipping cocktails as they shared their thoughts on how the new economic plan would improve trade throughout the region. Roger Warren, the American Secretary of State and a college friend of Amanda's father, stood nearby and offered his opinions when asked. Tomorrow, he would attend the signing of the agreement between San Rimini, Greece, and the Balkan nations.

So long as nothing goes wrong tonight.

Every minute, another VIP entered through the foyer's ornate entry doors and passed Amanda's position. A representative of the World Bank and a prominent member of Croatia's Sabor—its legislature—began a discussion that was quickly joined by two representatives of San Rimini's economic council. Each of them had an air that spoke of the economic power they wielded in their home country.

Amanda tried to take in the faces. She and Marco had spent as much time learning who was who as they did going over his talk and reviewing the economic plan. She discreetly withdrew her phone from her handbag to check for any last-minute messages from Marco. So far, nothing. She glanced at the time, then tucked the phone out of sight.

Within minutes, Marco would stroll through the same doors, ready to lead his guests to dinner in the elegant dining room and convincingly talk about how improved economic relations between nations could ensure long-term stability in the region. Or so she hoped. He'd done well in their brief practice session, but as she studied the dignitaries around her, and noted that a few reporters were doing the same, her nerves began to get the better of her.

As a tuxedoed waiter passed her bearing a silver tray filled with miniature quiche, Amanda wondered how Marco would cope with the pressure. None of them fazed him individually. One on one, over a beer or a game of cards or darts, she was certain he'd impress them with his charm, just as he'd impressed her.

But as a group, each angling to speak to him with a well-crafted agenda in mind, she wasn't sure how he would do. Would he let his discomfort get the better of him and say or do something inappropriate? Or worse, would he disappear entirely for several minutes, fighting to get his thoughts together, as he'd done during Antony and Jennifer's wedding?

Federico, Isabella, or Antony would thrive hosting such an important dinner. But Marco? She fervently hoped the experience he'd gained at yesterday's event would serve him well tonight.

Personally, she didn't want him to lose confidence in himself after he'd come so far with his lessons. Professionally, she knew she'd answer to the king if Marco failed.

Amanda took a deep breath, then accepted a glass of champagne from a member of the waitstaff when she stopped near Amanda's elbow with a tray. Within a few hours, Amanda would know if her lessons were as effective as the king expected. And she'd know if Marco diTalora would make—or break—her career.

"Prince Marco!" The feminine voice came from behind her, causing Amanda to spin around to determine its source. Eliza Schipani glided by, meeting Marco just as he crossed the threshold to the reception hall. Amanda cringed. Jennifer claimed the woman was intelligent and kind, but Marco hadn't gotten his bearings yet. The last thing he needed was to confront the bubbly Eliza.

Amanda had apparently worried for nothing, because Marco looked at the blonde with a hundred-watt smile on his face.

"Eliza, I'm so glad you could make it." His voice dropped so low Amanda could barely hear. "I understand you're declaring your candidacy for parliament tomorrow. Congratulations."

Taking the blonde's hand, he kissed it with such smooth grace Amanda would believe he had kissed the hands of a thousand important women at a thousand different state functions—if she didn't know otherwise. When he released Eliza Schipani's hand, his gaze drifted to meet Amanda's for a brief moment.

She shot him a look she hoped said, *you can do it.* His eyes flashed in understanding before he turned his attention back to the blonde in front of him.

"Why, thank you, Your Highness. It's my understanding that part of the economic agreement involves facilitating the exchange of medical research throughout the region. Improved access to the latest research for both doctors and patients is a big part of my health plan. It's imperative if we wish to improve our citizens' overall quality of life."

"I'm sure voters will find you quite persuasive on that point."

She smiled, then accepted a glass of champagne from the same woman who'd offered one to Amanda. "Speaking of persuasive, apparently I'm not. I still don't have a firm commitment from you about speaking at the San Rimini Health Affairs Conference next month. You know I'm chairing the event, and I'd be honored—"

"Of course. I'd be happy to. If you'd like to contact my assistant, she can check my agenda. So long as I'm not booked elsewhere, you can count on me."

Eliza looked as if she might drop her drink. They continued to chat for another minute, and when Marco took his leave to speak to a government official from Serbia, the excited smile on Eliza's face spoke volumes.

Amanda bit back a smile of her own. If the way he handled Eliza Schipani was any indication, Marco would do fine.

Amanda slipped away, spending the rest of the cocktail hour circulating through the reception hall, discreetly assessing the guests. When the dinner bell rang, however, Marco appeared at her elbow.

"I think it's going well so far."

She took stock of him: his tailored tuxedo, the angle of his tie, his smoothed-down hair. Even his grin showed confidence and poise. "Seems like it. If it's not patronizing to say so, I'm proud of you."

"I haven't gotten to the speech yet."

She resisted the urge to touch his arm. Too many eyes followed him, and too many questions would be asked. Thus far, few of the guests had even noticed her.

Marco must have felt the same because the flash of steam in his gaze was enough to make her insides melt. Did he have to be so handsome? So enticing?

"You won't be able to sit with me," he said. "I hadn't even thought of that."

She gave a slight shake of the head, but was secretly thrilled that he wanted her nearby. "You don't need me. You have it memorized."

"It's not that."

At that moment, the Greek economic minister, who stood behind Marco, raised his voice enough for Amanda to hear.

"The current refugee crisis puts a tremendous strain on the entire region. If we do not have a firm plan with deadlines to alleviate the problem as part of this package, what's to ensure its success? Why, the very foundation—"

Another man, heavy set, whom Amanda recognized as a representative from Slovenia, seemed agitated by the Greek's statement. "Of course the refugee problem is of concern, but don't you believe the current program to—"

Before she could cue him in, Marco took the initiative and turned to the Greek. "Mr. Theopholus, I believe you will be seated beside me. Have you found your place yet?"

"No, but—"

"Ah, I see Secretary Warren." He leaned toward the Slovenian representative, but aimed a pointed look at the American. "Mr. Jankovic, Secretary Warren has been anxious to talk to you. He wished to discuss the possibility of using Slovenia as the site of his follow-up meeting on the economic accords."

"Thank you, I'll try to catch him now." The Slovenian quickly excused himself and headed for the Secretary of State.

Once he was safely away, Marco returned his attention to the Greek, who now stood looking at Amanda. She tried to give Marco a look to indicate that she needed an introduction, but for a moment, he froze.

"Your Highness, I don't believe I've made the acquaintance," the Greek hinted.

Amanda saw Marco swallow. *Oh, no.* After all he'd accomplished, he couldn't let his nerves get to him now. Not after what he'd just done. And not over *her.* This was such a nothing moment compared to everything else.

"I apologize," he finally said. "This is Ms. Amanda Hutton. She has recently joined my diplomatic staff. Ms. Hutton, this is the Honorable Ari Theopholus of Greece."

Diplomatic staff? It was common knowledge that Marco had a driver and an assistant. Security if he wanted it. But a *diplomatic staff?* She tried not to look amused by the prince's description of her job as the broad-shouldered Greek took her hand.

"Ms. Hutton, a pleasure."

"Likewise."

Marco urged the minister toward his seat. "Dinner is about to start. We should head inside. By the way, I forgot to mention that I met your wife while skiing at Zermatt last year. She was there with her sister. She's quite accomplished. Do you ski as well?"

"I do."

Amanda forced back a laugh as Marco guided the man to the front of the state dining room, the two of them debating the merits of various ski resorts as they walked. She strolled through the room, searching for her name on the place cards at the long table. When she located it at one of the corners, about as far from Marco as she could be, a thought occurred to her.

If he continued to demonstrate such skills, her job tenure would never last the full three months. She could be home in a matter of weeks. The idea of spending the next two months, at least, in San Rimini had seemed a done deal. But if she were honest with herself, she should have realized it wasn't a given; only the salary was guaranteed.

She took her seat as waiters moved around her, filling crystal glasses so guests could toast the pending economic deal. Soon, Marco's voice echoed through the room, thanking everyone for their hard work, then extolling the merits of the plan and the manner in which it would bring together the countries surrounding the Adriatic Sea. Amanda hardly heard the words. Instead she closed her eyes, trying to memorize the silken timbre of his voice, the sound of the crystal glasses clinking around her, the breathless hush of the guests as they listened to the prince's every word. Deep in her soul, she knew this dinner would be her last.

Marco was intelligent, and he knew how to read social cues. Even if he were more comfortable in smaller groups than large ones, once he made it through tonight, he'd improve by leaps and bounds. He wouldn't need her.

Eventually, King Eduardo would introduce an appropriate, connected woman to Marco, someone local and perhaps even titled to stand by his side as he fulfilled his royal role. Someone who would make him a good partner, who would be a good mother to his children...and that someone would not be her. *Couldn't* be her.

Deep in her heart, she knew it would never work. She'd only cause him pain.

She'd known, for years, that if she had a serious relationship, one that went beyond a few dates and casual sex, it had to be with a certain type of man. Likely an older man. Someone who supported her career, and who didn't want children. Perhaps someone who already had them from a previous relationship.

Not Marco diTalora.

She opened her eyes as applause filled the room. Marco took his seat, and waiters approached from behind to set the salad course before the guests. Amanda hazarded a glance at the prince, and found him looking right at her. A flash of unbridled desire lit his face, every bit as potent as the look he'd given her seconds before his mouth had descended on hers in the library that afternoon. But there was something else to his gaze—a need than ran deeper than mere desire. He wanted her there, beside him. And not just to cheer him on during his speech.

In anyone else, she'd call it a look of love.

Her breath caught as she absorbed the impact of his look, sure she had to be mistaken. But then Secretary Warren said something that demanded the prince's attention, and Marco turned away before she could decide.

CHAPTER 10

MARCO WANTED to pump his fist with the excitement of a World Cup champion even before he and Amanda ducked into the library following the departure of the last guest. He hadn't experienced such a thrill since receiving his Princeton acceptance years ago. He'd known the minute he read the line beginning, 'We are pleased to offer you a position in the class...' that his life would never be the same. He'd be free of the palace routine, able to explore the outside world as normal people did. He'd spend time with those who didn't know or care about his life in San Rimini, people who spoke to him with no ulterior motives.

A whole new world opened to him that day.

Just as a whole new world opened to him today, in the very halls he'd once been so grateful to flee. He'd finally found the key in Amanda Hutton. She made him feel he could spread his wings without having to run away from his name.

The realization made his head spin and his heart want to burst. How could he have walked out on her this morning? How could he have believed it was idiocy to kiss her? He'd done what his heart and his gut knew to be right.

As he took in the sight of her elegant black gown and flushed face, he knew he'd never want to host another function with her sitting at the far end of the table. He wanted her beside him.

"What did I tell you? You pulled it off!" Amanda said once the library doors closed behind them. "Prince Federico and Princess Isabella couldn't have done any better, and they've handled these affairs for years."

"You think?"

"Can't you hear the pride in your own voice?" Amanda leaned against one of the yellow chairs, her face glowing with the same sense of accomplishment he felt all the way to his soul. "I'm so happy for you, Prince Marco."

He spread his arms wide, allowing himself to revel in his moment of accomplishment. "Did you see Eliza during the cocktail hour? She nearly choked on her champagne when I accepted her invitation to speak. And the representative from Slovenia—the way I eased him toward Secretary Warren when the Greek minister questioned the plan as it regards war refugees? My father won't believe it."

He strode toward Amanda and smacked his palm against the yellow fabric of the chair. "And the speech! I swear, if you'd bet me a month ago that I'd successfully host a dinner as important as this one, and that I'd actually get an adrenaline rush from it, I wouldn't have taken that bet. Never in a million years. But it was easy!"

He surprised himself by pulling Amanda into his arms, then swinging her—fancy dress be damned—around the richly appointed library. He laughed at the ridiculousness of it, then stopped and set her down, still in the circle of his embrace.

"Prince Marco! This isn't—"

"Appropriate? The hell with appropriate. You wrote at least half of that speech, and it sounded—it felt—like me. You made sure I absorbed enough information that I could handle a dinner sitting next to the American Secretary of State of all people, and not blow it. Because of you, I avoided every stumbling block that landed in front of me, and managed to do something I would have sworn was impossible."

He expected her to chastise him, to push him away as she had that afternoon, but instead, an unstoppable smile lifted her face. He closed his eyes for a moment, wanting to memorize that expression: a mixture of unabashed joy and certainty. Certainty in him. She believed in him, and that unconditional support made her incredibly, irresistibly sexy.

"*You* made it easy," he added, still amazed at Amanda's skill. How she'd gotten him to this point in such a short time astounded him. "I never could have done this without you."

He tightened his hold on her so she couldn't escape, then lifted her off her feet to brush his lips against hers. Before he could stop himself, he parted Amanda's soft lips with his own, tasting her warmth and a hint of the wine they'd been served for dessert. With a moan, he slid his tongue against hers in an age-old, erotic dance that showed her the true extent of his gratitude.

A soft sigh escaped her as she returned his kiss, hesitantly at first, then with deeper passion. Her arms wound tightly around his neck, her breasts pressed against his chest, and even though her feet had to be off the floor, he couldn't bring himself to put her down. Amanda felt too warm and firm against his body. Too perfect a fit.

Finally, she eased her mouth from his to whisper, "I know you said 'the hell with appropriate,' but we both know this is a mistake. We have to stop. What if your father comes back from the hospital dedication? He'll want to see you to hear how it went and to congratulate you. And you're still my student. For the time being, at least."

He set her down within the circle of his arms. She put a tentative hand on his lapel, but didn't push him away.

"It's not that I'm not enjoying this," she hastily added. "Which I'm pretty sure you can tell. But you have to know it could easily come back to bite us both."

The sensation of having Amanda's small hand flat against his chest, her lower body still pressed to his, brought forth a mental image of what it'd be like to have her in his bed, entangling his body with hers, making love to her for hours. He was dead certain she'd shake off the mantle of propriety then.

Apparently reading his mind—once again—she leaned back from his embrace.

"Your Highness—"

"Oh for the love of...when will you finally start calling me Marco? And right now, I don't care about my father interrupting. Or anyone else," his words came out raspy.

"But—"

He let go of her and strode to the library door. "In fact, I think it's high time I taught you a few lessons. First lesson, dear student, is to lock the door when you don't wish to be interrupted."

He spun the lock home, then crossed back to her in three quick strides. He ran his hand along the side of her face, forcing her to meet his eyes and see how much he wanted her. Instead, he was knocked back by the desire he saw in hers.

"Second," he instructed, "if you want something, the proper thing to do is grab it while you have the opportunity." Sliding his hands around her hips, he lifted her easily, took a few steps across the library's antique rug, then deposited her bottom-first on his great-grandmother's cherry desk.

"This is definitely *not* proper," she protested. "And you know I can't call you Marco. It wouldn't—"

He captured her lips with his own to quiet her. Wedging himself against the desk between her legs, he reached down to grab the hem of her evening gown, then slipped the beaded fabric high enough to allow him to caress one perfect thigh.

One of her high heels fell to the floor, bumping his calf as it went, then he heard the sharp intake of her breath. But instead of fighting him, she reached to his shoulders and shoved at his tuxedo jacket, wrestling it to the floor. Her hands moved to his back, her fingers leaving fiery trails along his skin even through the fabric of his dress shirt. He could lose himself in this woman. Wanted to lose himself in her. For once in his life, the risks of loving a woman didn't matter to him. He wanted this one moment with Amanda, even if it meant a lifetime of hurt would follow.

He pulled her even closer, so they were hip to hip, then kissed her slowly and deeply, enjoying the effortless way they moved together. He trailed kisses to her throat, then back to her luscious mouth, as heat continued to build between them. Her legs tightened around him, and he heard her second shoe hit the floor.

He couldn't get enough of her. He pressed a kiss to her temple and inhaled the scent of her hair, then whispered, "I've been fascinated by you from the moment we met. Obsessed with you since we walked through the rose garden the night of Antony and Jennifer's wedding. But I was afraid to let this happen."

Amanda's fingers had been in his hair, but she shifted to capture his chin between her thumb and fingers. Her eyes held the glazed look of passion, and her breathing came in an erratic rhythm. Her gaze dropped to his mouth, then she closed her eyes. "We shouldn't let it happen now. For a number of reasons."

He waited for her to open her eyes and look into his, then smiled, hoping to reassure her. "You saw how it went tonight. Perhaps I don't need you as my tutor any longer. Perhaps I need you in another role."

She blanched. "Don't say that. Jennifer told me that your father has considered arranging a marriage for you at some point. And that when he mentioned it, you didn't object. A marriage to someone more appropriate—"

"No," he told her. "Absolutely not. If my father didn't learn his lesson with Antony, he'll learn it now. I didn't object at the time because I didn't believe he'd actually do it, and if he tried, I didn't care. It didn't seem like a risk. Now I do care. I think you know that. You understand me, and you anticipate me. You convinced me that I can accomplish more than I've allowed myself to believe I can." He paused a beat, running his thumb along her jaw, before adding, "I'm utterly fascinated by you, Amanda Hutton. I want to spend time with you. I want to understand you and to be as important in your world as you already are in mine. Tonight, when you couldn't sit with me during the dinner, all of that hit me at once. I just knew."

How could he possibly explain the empty feeling he'd had at seeing her relegated to the far end of the table, as if she meant nothing to him? He'd wanted her there by his side, his partner in every way. In the seat of honor.

He blew out a hard breath. "I've been wrong, Amanda. Perhaps some things, and some women, are worth going beyond the limits you put on yourself. They're worth the risk."

He dipped his head to kiss her again, but Amanda eased back on the desk, dodging him. "Prince Marco—"

"Marco. Please."

Her gaze dropped to his chest. She splayed her hands there, and after what seemed an interminable moment, she brought them to his shoulders and lifted her chin. At the same moment he registered that her lips were wet from his kisses, she whispered, "Marco."

The two syllables undid him.

SHE KNEW what would happen before his name left her lips.

When she'd used it accidentally following his near fall at the pier, he'd picked up on it instantly and teased her. There was no amusement now.

"Come with me," he said.

His fingers laced through hers, his grip tight. She didn't question it until they were on the far side of the library from where they usually worked and he used his free hand to pull on one of the curtains.

She frowned, afraid that speaking would break the spell between them. Then his fingers found a spot between the curtain's edge and a library shelf and he pushed.

On the opposite side of the shelf, she heard a click. Marco dropped the curtain, then guided her to the wall where she'd heard the sound. The chair rail now jutted two finger widths from the wall. Marco touched it and the entire wall swung open.

"A hidden door? I would never have guessed." When she'd lived in Italy, her parents had taken her on tours of castles in several countries. Guides had thrilled their visitors by showing off entrances to secret passageways, but never had she seen one as well disguised as this.

"Better than a hidden door. A hidden staircase." He flicked on a light, then eased her inside, closing the door behind them. As they climbed, he said, "It leads to the hallway outside my residence and Isabella's."

"You haven't used it when you've come to our sessions." She imagined he'd have loved to be purposely late, then pop out of the wall to frighten her.

"My parents dissuaded us from using it. I haven't in years." He pointed to a burned out bulb. "I doubt anyone has. Aside from the family, only the head of security knows it exists. It's narrow enough that it was left off all blueprints without anyone questioning it."

They reached the top in seconds. After listening at the door, Marco opened it slowly and scanned the hall. They hurried its length, passing what he whispered was the entrance to Princess Isabella's apartment. Amanda's heart thrummed in her ears as he punched in the key code to open an identical entrance at the end of the hall.

And then they were in. He didn't reach for the switch. Instead, he spun her, pulled her body flush to his, and lowered his head to kiss her throat. The sensation of his hot mouth at her pulse and his hands bracketing her waist was nothing short of divine.

Her head fell back until it rested against the wall. Every part of her wanted him. Here, in the dark of his room, where they were equals. Where she wasn't his tutor, and he wasn't a prince.

His teeth grazed the spot he'd kissed, then his hand slipped under the spaghetti strap of her dress.

A blissful sigh left her lips. His hold on her tightened. She felt him growing hard against her, and suddenly, she needed to kiss him. She lifted his head and pulled his mouth to hers for a hungry kiss.

The moment couldn't last, but she refused to think about it now. For once in her life, she was going to turn off the part of her brain that always questioned, always thought two steps ahead. She was going to make love to the man who'd charmed her in the back of the

Range Rover on the way to a royal wedding, and who'd enthralled her more and more every moment since.

Still kissing her, he eased her through the apartment. She could see nothing, but he moved with surety until she felt the sweep of bedcovers against her leg. He gave her a final, lingering kiss, then sat on the bed, pulling her so she stood between his knees. A hint of moonlight came through the curtains, allowing her to see the outline of his face, but not his expression. His hands raked her sides, and he lowered the other strap of her gown, then eased it to her waist. There was a hitch in his voice when he murmured, "No bra."

"Built into the dress."

"Modern marvel."

"It will need to unzip before it goes further."

"I'll get to that."

Then his mouth was on her breast, his hands firm at the base of her rib cage, holding her steady as heat lanced through her. She swore with the pleasure of it. When he moved to her other breast, his knees shifted, trapping her.

Her fingers went from his shoulders to his collar. What little she could feel of his skin radiated heat. She fumbled for the first button. "I want your shirt off yesterday. Preferably faster."

She felt his wicked rumble of laughter against her breast as much as she heard it. Several seconds elapsed before he released her to work his way out of his clothing. She watched, her breathing shallow, until he reached the point where he needed to free his wrists. Since she had the better angle, she made quick work of the task, and dropped the shirt to the floor.

Even in the dark, he was stunning. As she reached for him, he located the zipper at the back of her waist and maneuvered it along its track until the dress was loose enough to fall to the floor.

Before she could draw another breath, he pulled her on top of him so they were finally skin to skin. "I've wanted you from the moment we met," he whispered between kisses. "I'm glad it took until tonight."

The emotion in his voice told her exactly what he meant. He wanted her in his bed, but he wanted it to be special, to have meaning.

Their kisses and caresses grew fiercer, hungrier. Her hips moved against his, and he groaned in response, then flipped her so his weight held her pinned to the bed.

"You feel amazing," she whispered.

"Just wait." He trailed his way down her body, kissing her stomach, then moving lower. He freed her of her panties, then kissed her again, his arm wrapping around her thigh. She nearly came off the bed at the brush of his tongue, then his teeth, then his tongue again.

"Marco."

He smiled against her. "Say it again."

She did. Moments later, he levered himself forward until his forehead was a breath from hers. He'd jettisoned his pants and she hadn't even noticed, she'd been so lost in desire. Having him naked, lying on top of her, felt right. She ached for him to shift his hips, to have him inside her, but her sense of responsibility pierced the fog. "I'm on the pill, so pregnancy isn't a concern, but—"

"I've got it," he said, reaching for his night table. Moments later, he smoothed her hair from her face. The break in the curtains allowed a shard of light to hit so she could finally see his expression. Pure wonderment. Amanda thought her heart might burst. This man did it for her. There was no other way to describe it.

She rose to give him a soft, slow kiss, one she hoped conveyed the all-encompassing emotion.

A low rumble of contentment came from the back of Marco's throat, and his hand slipped between them. A beat later, he was inside her. She shuddered at the sensation. Their gentle kiss turned passionate as overwhelming, primal need surged in each of them. He eased back, then surged inside her again. Instinctively, she picked up the rhythm. There was no awkwardness, no questioning. They fit. Later, when the hard coil of her orgasm released, he captured her moan with a kiss that left her reeling. Moments later, his body quaked, hard, and his fist ground into the pillow near her head. He groaned her name on a powerful exhale before slowly collapsing on top of her.

His heart pounded against hers. She held him in the stillness as their skin cooled. Carefully, he shifted to lie beside her, quickly dealing with the condom before gathering her into his embrace.

Surrounded by his arms, his chest, his breath in her hair...never had her soul felt so at peace, yet so full of fire and elation. She could breathe in his scent and revel in the feel of him for a long, long time.

He felt it, too. She didn't need him to say the words to know it to be true.

She wasn't sure how long they remained wrapped together before he whispered, "Stay."

She pressed her back into his chest. She wanted to stay more than anything.

Even knowing she couldn't.

CHAPTER 11

MARCO PRESSED his lips to her shoulder. She tasted like heaven. He said it again. "Stay."

Her fingertips slid along the inside of his arm, prickling his skin. "If I do, everyone will know."

He smiled without lifting his mouth from the spot he'd kissed. "I'm not sure I care. This is worth everything."

The vibration of her laugh carried through her back. A beat later, he felt the change in her.

"Your mind is racing," he whispered. "Something is bothering you all of a sudden. What is it?"

"I'm that transparent?"

"No. But we seem to be getting to know each other better, so—"

He grinned as she gave his leg a half-hearted swat. Still, he needed to know what caused the shift. He kept his voice light and asked again, "What is it, Amanda?"

"Well, Marco," she made a point of saying his name without the title attached, and continued to drag her fingers back and forth along his arm. Before she finished her sentence, he wondered if she needed a profession of his adoration, given the emotional and physical intensity of what passed between them. More than at any other point in his life, he was willing to make one.

"Yes?"

"When we were in the library, just before we came upstairs, you said 'some women are worth the risk.'"

"I said that you are worth the risk."

She wiggled against him, but remained undeterred. "Exactly what risk were you talking about? It didn't strike me as fear that your father will disapprove of me. It struck me as a fear that came from within you. What had you afraid to let things happen between us? Or with any other woman? Because that's what I heard in your statement. That you view having a relationship as taking a great personal risk. When you said it was worth everything...well, that made me remember what you'd said in the library."

So, she wasn't fishing for the magic words, which made him feel them all the more. Still, he'd rather talk about what he felt for her than discuss his mother's death any day.

"It's nothing important," he said, but even to his own hearing, his words weren't convincing.

She pushed to her elbow, then rolled so she faced him. She took a long inhale, then tucked one arm under her head and placed the other on his chest. "Tell me anyway."

He should have known Amanda wouldn't let him dodge the issue. "This is going to sound immensely ridiculous—"

"I don't care."

"Fine, fine." He rolled his eyes. At some point he'd have to tell her anyway. "If you want the emotional, psychobabble explanation, I've been wary of getting too close to anyone ever since my mother died. Deep down, part of me has been afraid that they could die, too. I know that's not logical. I suspect it's a fear that was injected deep into my brain in the days that surrounded her funeral. Evolutionary protection."

She was quiet, letting him turn over his jumbled thoughts until he could explain. Finally, he said, "When my father suggested an arranged marriage, I think that's why I didn't object. First, I knew I had a time buffer. He was far more concerned with Antony. Second, while I didn't exactly want an arranged marriage, I knew having one meant I would never be hurt the way my father was when my mother passed away."

He forced a grin to his face, then made himself meet her gaze. "Told you it was ridiculous. None of this was conscious thought, not really. Just a promise I made to myself not to end up like my father. He wasn't himself for a long time after her death."

"It's not ridiculous at all."

"In any case, didn't you tell me that the way to get past my fears was to jump in with both feet? It worked for the dinner tonight. I've discovered it works in this case, too." He reached around her waist, locking her body once more to his, then lifted her thigh to his hip and massaged the silken skin of her leg in a promise of things to come. "Besides, you don't look like you're in danger of imminent death. In fact, I happen to know that you are very much alive. I want to see what the future holds for us."

Amanda edged away from him again, and in the dim light, he saw her blink, as if gathering her emotions.

"Amanda?" What had he said?

A sickening feeling spread through his gut and his heart lurched. "You're not ill, are you? After what I just said—"

She shook her head. "It's not that."

A wave of relief swept through him. "Thank God. Then what's going on?"

Amanda seemed more averse to saying whatever it was than he'd been about discussing his mother.

"It can't be that bad, Amanda. Just spit it out."

Her fingers curled into the sheet. "My mother and my aunt—"

From somewhere behind him, his phone vibrated against the floor. He hadn't taken it out of his pants before kicking them off.

"Do you need to get that?"

"No."

She angled her head. Before the boat race and before tonight's dinner, she'd reminded him to shut off his phone. He'd told her that it would vibrate for immediate family members or the head of security, and that those calls would likely only come for important matters, since they knew his schedule. For all other calls, his phone was set to silent.

When the phone stopped, he asked, "What about your mother and aunt? I know they both had cancer. Is there something else?"

The phone vibrated again. Marco swore under his breath. Why now, of all times? He pleaded with Amanda, "What about them?"

"Now is not the time. You need to get that."

"*What?*" Marco demanded. He could hear in her voice that she was trying to stay unemotional and failing. "I'm not touching that phone until you tell me. Whatever is going through your mind, it's important."

"Fine," Amanda said. "You want to know what's wrong? I'm sure you, of all people, are aware that certain cancers can run in families. I had genetic testing done last year. Turns out I have the same mutated gene for the disease as my mother and aunt. In fact, I have multiple mutated genes. My odds of developing breast or ovarian cancer are higher than either of theirs were."

His heart constricted, and his dread must have shown on his face, because she continued, undeterred, "That's why you can never, ever have a future with me, Marco. There might not *be* a future. I have more appointments scheduled, but I have a lot of decisions to make. Many of those decisions may mean I don't have children. And even if I take the most aggressive preventive actions I can, I could still end up with the disease. Is that what you wanted to hear?"

"Amanda—" The crushing weight in his chest bordered on the unbearable. It wasn't possible. After all this time, to have found a woman whom he could actually *love*, someone who made him reconsider his promise to himself, then to find out...he ached for her. He ached for himself.

His phone vibrated again.

"There's an emergency, Marco. There has to be." She exhaled and gave him a mild push. "I'm sorry I blew up, but it's...look, apparently my emotions are in overdrive at the moment. People should never have these conversations immediately following sex, because things are said that shouldn't be. I'll be fine in a few minutes. You need to get your phone. That's more important."

He swore aloud, then rolled to search for the offending phone. "This conversation's not over, Amanda," he said, then answered with a "Yes?"

"Miroslav says you went to the library with Amanda Hutton after the dinner." It was Isabella.

"Yes, I—"

"Are you still there? I need to see you."

He hesitated. He couldn't say no, or she'd insist on coming to his room. There'd been no hello, no questions about how dinner went. Something major had happened. "Where are you?" he asked. Maybe he could go to her.

"About to leave my room. Stay put."

She clicked off without saying goodbye. It occurred to him then that Isabella was supposed to be in Venice. He swore aloud.

"What?"

"Isabella's on her way to the library. Wants to see me."

Amanda gasped. "My shoes are still down there. And my handbag."

He scooped her dress from the floor, shook it to ensure it was right side out, then held it by the straps. "Step in. We'll go the way we came."

She kicked her legs over the bed, pulled up the dress, then turned so he could zip the back. While he grabbed his clothes and dressed, she found her panties and shimmied into them. "Won't she see us in the hall?"

"Hurry. We'll wait by the door and listen for her to leave, then we'll run for it. We should beat her downstairs. It'll take her quite a bit longer."

Less than two minutes later, Marco opened the hidden door and ushered Amanda into the library. While she located her shoes, he shut off the staircase light and ensured the door was closed.

"Here," he said as he approached her. "Look at me."

After she wiggled her feet into her high heels, he smoothed her hair into place, then eyeballed her dress to make sure nothing was out of place.

"She'll know—"

"You look fine," he assured her. "Me?"

He gave his shirt a firm tuck into the waist of his slacks while she inspected him. "Probably too good."

The library door rattled. He'd forgotten he'd locked it.

"Whoops," Amanda muttered, glancing in that direction.

He gestured toward the desk chair and whispered, "Sit."

"Sorry," he called, then jogged across the room and flipped the lock, frantically trying to come up with a good explanation. He swung it open to find himself staring into reddened eyes.

He knew instantly that Isabella didn't need an explanation. She didn't care about the door or why it might be locked.

"Mi scusi." Her face paled as she looked from him to Amanda, then back to him again. "I hate to interrupt, but you need to see Federico. Antony's gone and I—I..."

Marco did a double take. Isabella's every-hair-in-its-place style had slipped, leaving loose tendrils tumbling from her bun onto her neck and shoulders. Her suit jacket was wrinkled down the front, as if she'd been slumped in a chair or had been holding something tight against her. Either way, it was completely out of character.

He cupped her arm above the elbow and drew her into the library. "What happened? Why aren't you in Venice? I didn't think you were coming home until tomorrow at the earliest."

Isabella glanced at Amanda, then looked back to Marco. "You must not have heard."

"Heard what?"

His sister swallowed so hard he could hear it. "Father called me earlier this evening and told me to take the helicopter home right away. It's Federico. He won't talk to anyone."

Marco took a deep breath, forcing himself not to shake the story out of Isabella. Federico wanting privacy was no reason to drag Isabella home from Venice, or to send her running through the palace to find him in the middle of the night. "Isabella, *what happened?*"

"It's Lucrezia." Isabella sniffled, the first time he'd heard her make such a sound since childhood. "A few hours ago, while you were hosting the dinner and Father was at the dedication ceremony for the new hospital wing, she died."

Isabella choked on the last word, then buried her face in her hands. Died?

He couldn't have heard right. Lucrezia was in her early thirties, only a few years older than Marco. Aside from a recent spate of headaches—which were understandable given that she was raising two active toddler sons—she was perfectly healthy. She ate well, took the occasional vacation with Federico to manage her stress levels, and came from a family of fitness enthusiasts.

He'd chatted with her on the staircase yesterday, and hadn't noticed a thing amiss.

"Lucrezia is dead?" His body went numb, his mind not quite absorbing Isabella's words.

Isabella nodded, then puffed out a long breath and lifted her head to look at him again. She was fighting to hold herself together. "Father went from one wing of Royal Memorial to another when he heard she'd been admitted. He and Federico just returned to the palace. I didn't get many details. Father said Federico refused to talk about it and went straight to his apartment."

"I'll stay with your sister," Amanda's voice came from behind Marco, quiet but reassuring. He hadn't even heard her approach. She put a hand on his back, gently guiding him toward the door. "Do what you can for your brother."

He blinked, then went. Deal with the emergency first. Think about it later.

Marco took the marble stairs leading to Federico's apartment by twos. Then down the long hall, past the surprised guard. Of all the family, Federico kept the earliest hours. His boys, Arturo and Paolo, were awake early and went to bed early, so Federico and Lucrezia organized their schedules around them. At this time of night, it was rare to see a guest, even a member of the family, approach this wing.

Isabella was right, though. Federico shouldn't be alone. The diTalora siblings had never been the type to turn to others in time of need, especially Federico. Federico liked to work through his difficulties in private. But Marco would be damned if he'd let his older brother shut him out now.

"Federico?" Marco knocked on the door to the apartment. When there was silence, he called louder. "*Federico!*"

It was a full minute before he heard what might be footsteps on the other side of the heavy door. No one answered, though, so he pounded again.

"I am going to sleep, Marco. The guard was to inform you that I'd retired." A hollow, strained edge tinged Federico's normally formal tone. "I shall speak with you tomorrow."

Stubborn man. Marco tried the handle and found the door locked. Of course it was.

"Marco, please—"

"If you don't open this door in the next minute, I'll force Chiara or Miroslav to give me the code. You know I will."

Marco held his breath, straining to hear through the thick wood. Finally, the door cracked open. His older brother's eyes were bloodshot, his forehead etched with worry lines. He wore a pair of charcoal pinstriped pants Marco recognized were part of a custom-tailored suit, along with a light gray dress shirt. No jacket. His shoes were still on. Wordlessly, he urged Marco inside.

When the door was closed, he said softly, "It's true, then."

"I—I have sent Arturo and Paolo to Father's apartments for the evening. He is keeping them occupied until I can figure out a way to say…to tell them…"

Marco pulled Federico to him, and found he nearly had to support his always-in-control elder brother to keep the man from falling over.

"I don't know what to say. I'm in shock. I'm so sorry, Federico."

"As am I," Federico replied into his shoulder, even as he tried to straighten himself, to wrest back control of his emotions. He gestured to his slacks. "I had hoped to come to the dinner, at least for a brief time, but thankfully I stayed here. Lucrezia wouldn't have made it to the hospital. She would have been alone."

Marco urged his brother to the living room and into a chair. Once Federico was seated, Marco went to the kitchenette, located a bottle of aspirin, and filled a glass with water. He took the chair next to Federico's, pressed two aspirin into his brother's hand, then set the water on the side table. He waited while Federico slugged the drink and the aspirin. The fact Federico didn't argue spoke volumes about his brother's state of mind. Typically, he'd have politely refused both the pills and the drink.

"Was it related to her headache?"

"She had a brain aneurysm." Federico was quiet, and Marco resisted the urge to fill the void. The fact Federico was sitting here, facing him, meant he'd eventually talk. When he finally did, it was as if he were seeing the events in his mind's eye and reciting them.

"We didn't realize until it was too late. Lucrezia told me this morning that it was another migraine—a bad one—which is why I decided to bow out of dinner. But then, this afternoon, she said it was worse than usual and that it felt different. I could tell by looking at her that it was worse. I told her I wanted to call her physician. While I was getting the number, she suddenly felt nauseous and started vomiting. I took her directly to the hospital and called ahead so he could meet us at the emergency room." Federico paused, steadying himself, then said, "Within minutes of our arrival she had back-to-back seizures."

His eyes welled with tears, but he rubbed them away quickly with his index finger and thumb and shook his head, regaining his composure. "They did a scan and were prepping her for emergency surgery when she passed away. There was nothing we could have done, according to the head of the emergency room. It happened so fast. If I had not witnessed it myself, I would not have believed it." His pained gaze met Marco's. "She was so full of life, Marco. So young. Younger than our mother, even."

Marco reached across the space between them to clasp his brother's shoulder. "Don't think about what happened at the hospital, or about our mother. It will only make you feel worse. Think about the love you and Lucrezia shared."

"But I must think of our mother, and the way Father was after her death. As for Lucrezia, I can't...." Federico ground his fist against his forehead. Marco let his brother have a moment as he tried to push his own memories of their mother from his mind. Images of those terrible final hours came to him against his will: of the late-night visit from her longtime private assistant, rousing him out of bed with a command to come to his parents' apartment. Of edging into the bedroom to see the king sitting stoically beside the bed, nursing a glass of whiskey and mumbling to himself that he was about to lose the only person who mattered to him. Of seeing his mother unconscious, and unaware, her skin hollow and gray as she took breaths so shallow her chest barely moved. Of feeling adrift in the days that followed that horrible night.

Marco shuddered. Returning his focus to his grieving brother, he prodded, "What were you going to say, Federico? You can't what?"

"I—" Federico let out a hollow laugh, then allowed his hand to drop to his lap. "For once in my life, I do not have the right words for the occasion." He exhaled, his body caving into the chair like a balloon with the air let out of it. "I suppose I should just say it point blank."

The polished elder prince looked around the empty bedroom, as if he expected someone might overhear, then turned back to face Marco. "I never loved Lucrezia. I have never admitted that, not even to myself, before today. But it's true. I did not love her."

"Of course you did," Marco argued, even though he knew the truth of Federico's words, and had always known. Now wasn't the time for Federico to fixate on it. "You can't—"

"No, Marco." Federico's expression left no doubt about his sincerity. "Lucrezia and I were essentially business partners. And friends, of course. Dear friends. But I did not love her as a man should love his wife."

Marco shook his head. Under Federico's cool, composed exterior, he had a heart as big as a bear's. Lucrezia, on the other hand, always seemed cool through and through. Their marriage had essentially been arranged—a series of dates set up by his parents and Lucrezia's family after they'd discussed the pair's suitability—and Federico had been happy to follow along. Marco distinctly remembered when

Federico told his parents over a family dinner that he'd proposed, and that it was "a good pairing for the country." Apparently it hadn't been so good for Federico.

"Why are you saying this now?" Marco asked. "And why to me?"

"Guilt, first and foremost." Federico massaged his temples, as if he thought he could rub out the night's events. "And I am telling you, Marco, because I could not imagine a worse feeling than the one I have now. It is worse than mourning a wife and lover. For the rest of my life, I will carry the knowledge that I cheated her."

"What? How?"

"I cheated her out of spending her life, as brief as it was, with someone who loved her completely. She deserved better. And I cannot undo that."

How could Federico possibly think that? If anything, he was the one who got cheated. "No, Federico. You were fulfilling a role you were born to, something you were duty-bound to do. Lucrezia knew that. Even if you didn't love her—and maybe you did, maybe you didn't—you were partners. Marriages have thrived on far less than what the two of you shared. Besides, Lucrezia was a grown woman when you met. It takes two to marry."

Marco gestured to a framed picture of the couple on the ledge above Federico's fireplace. Taken the day of Federico and Lucrezia's engagement, it had run in nearly every newspaper in the world. "She entered the marriage as willingly as you did, knowing all the pros and cons. She was happy to be part of the royal family, and for you to be part of hers. She loved Arturo and Paolo. I doubt she'd have made different decisions, even in hindsight. Don't for a minute think you cheated her."

Federico glanced at the engagement photograph, then sighed. "Perhaps. There are always those who wish to live such a life. Still, that does not make it right."

Marco glanced at the signet ring Federico always wore, the one their father had presented to him on his eighteenth birthday. Federico had done his duty as a member of the royal family, and he'd taken pride in it. It suited him. What could possibly be wrong with that?

From birth, the diTalora children had been told that their duty to their subjects was more important than any personal desires they might have. Their lives belonged to those they ruled; they had limited choice over their destinies. Federico had honored that lesson, maintaining a formal tone at all times, marrying someone from a well-respected family with deep roots in San Rimini, producing heirs, attending state functions...all without giving a thought to his own needs.

Federico, of all people, shouldn't blame himself for the choices he'd made in life. And not tonight, of all nights. There'd been many days where Marco felt his own life would be easier if he could toe the line as Federico did.

"I know this might be tough to believe," Marco finally said, "and maybe it's cold of me to say it to you now, but you did what was right for you at the time. In the long run, you'll realize that. You'll realize that you were better off for not having loved her, but for having been friends and partners and parents. You'll be better able to cope with her death, and you'll help your children cope better than our own father did."

Federico eyes flared in disgust. "And this, Marco, is why I make my confession to you. Of all people."

He felt his head jerk back. "I don't understand."

Federico pinned him with an iron-hard stare. "Because you have always been so certain you could avoid pain by avoiding love. It is not so. It will never be so. Pain is a fact of life. Not having love makes it worse." Federico shook his head, then slammed his hand against the arm of the chair and stood, his back ramrod straight as he strode to the far end of the room. He ran a hand over his chin, then turned to face Marco.

"You think I am not in pain? I am in terrible pain. Even if I am better equipped to help my children through this than Father was— and I'm not convinced I am—it will not be easy. They loved their mother as much as we loved ours."

"I don't doubt it. But you have a strong inner core, Federico. I've known it all my life, and your children know it, too. They know they can count on you."

"But what happens the day they realize my true feelings for their mother? Whether it happens when they are six years old or thirty-six, will they resent me any less than you resented the way Father retreated into himself in the days after our mother died?" He let out a sarcastic laugh. "I do not believe so. In fact, I think it will be worse. Much worse."

Federico grabbed a thick, leather-bound book off the top of a nearby end table. "This is my wedding album. It means a great deal to me, but it would mean so much more if I had truly loved Lucrezia. Look at these pictures, Marco. Look carefully. Then think about the photographs that will fill Antony and Jennifer's album. Think about what my children will see when they are old enough to view those albums side by side."

"Federico—"

Federico dropped the weighty album in Marco's lap. "You are at a crossroads. Now that you are home, you have decisions to make. Where do you wish your life to go? What approach will you take in pursuit of that life? When you marry, do you wish to have an album like mine to share with your children, when something as powerful as what Antony and Jennifer share is within your grasp?"

Marco started to argue, but hesitated. "What are you talking about? What's within my grasp?"

"Amanda Hutton, perhaps."

Marco ran his hand over Federico's album. "It's not like that."

Even as he denied it, he knew it was true. He loved Amanda. Less than a month had elapsed since they met, but he knew it. Tonight, when he'd watched her sitting at the end of the table during the dinner, and then when they'd shared his bed, he'd finally understood what drove Antony to take the risks he'd taken to marry Jennifer. But Marco wasn't sure he could make the leap Antony made. Jumping out of airplanes, rappelling down cliffs, skiing off-trail...the dangers to which Marco had willingly subjected himself over the years paled in comparison to the thought of giving his heart to Amanda, particularly considering what she had told him tonight.

She might die.

"No, Federico," he argued. "Even assuming I was head over heels in love with Amanda Hutton—which I'm absolutely not saying—it could never work. Not for me."

Federico smiled for the first time that evening. "I have walked past the library several times in the last few weeks. I have seen the way you look at her, Marco, when you believe no one is watching. I've never seen you look at another human being that way. Yet you act as though it is wrong for you to have such emotions. Why are you so afraid?"

"We don't need to talk about Amanda now. You have other things—"

Federico crossed his arms over his chest. "Do you have any idea how many people want to hire her, Marco? After Lucrezia heard that Amanda was working with you, she told me we should consider hiring her for Arturo and Paolo once her obligation with you was complete. I sent Father a message and asked if we could discuss it, but he told me that several friends of Amanda's father had heard of her employment here and inquired after her future availability. They'd each considered hiring her before, apparently, but now with the diTalora name on her résumé, they finally made the decision to move forward."

Marco wasn't surprised, given Amanda's skill. But he didn't understand Federico's point in telling him.

His confusion must have shown on his face, because Federico wrenched his mouth in exasperation. "If you believe you have all the time in the world to decide whether you are capable of giving yourself to Amanda, you are wrong. Pursue the opportunity that has been presented to you. Now. If you do not, she will be gone, and you will not be able to get her back. She will take it as disinterest." Federico gestured to the heavy book in Marco's lap. "If you follow my path, you will be no better off than I was on my wedding day. Or than I am now."

Marco stood, carefully holding Federico's album. "I appreciate the thought, Federico, but you don't understand—"

"I do understand. You are afraid to love, and you always have been. Given what happened with Mother and Father, I don't blame you. But think of it this way: what would Mother have wanted you to do?"

"That's not a fair question."

"No?" His brother gestured toward the door. "The next few days will be a whirlwind. Go to your room, get some sleep, and think about what I have said. I need to check on the children."

The set of Federico's jaw gave Marco the impression that his brother wouldn't tolerate any further discussion. He skimmed his fingers over the rich leather of Federico's wedding album, then held it out for his brother.

Federico waved him off. "Take it back to your apartment. I shall come for it later, when I can bear to look at it again. Until then, it will be of more use to you." A soft, self-deprecating laugh escaped him. "Perhaps you can redeem my mistakes in some small way by not repeating them yourself."

Marco doubted he'd find the album the least bit useful, but wasn't willing to add more stress to his brother's anguished night by arguing the point.

"All right." He grasped Federico's arm briefly. "Call me if you need me."

"And you call if you need me."

Marco let himself out of Federico's apartment, then strode through the empty hallways until he reached his father's wing. As he passed the guard and approached the door, he saw it was open. The vestibule was dark, but light filtered into it from the great room beyond. Apparently his father had hoped Federico would come. Then Marco heard the soft cadence of Isabella's voice, apparently reading a fairy tale to Federico's children. The boys' laughter followed, giving Marco pause.

There was nothing he could do for Arturo and Paolo tonight. He glanced back over his shoulder, debating, looking beyond the guard who stood watch in the hallway until the man cocked his head, puzzled.

"Prince Marco, *va bene?*"

He let out a deep breath. "No, nothing is all right. But we'll get through it. We always do."

The guard nodded and Marco headed toward his own apartment. Without thinking, he took a meandering route, needing to think and stretch his legs. On the ground floor, he entered a long marble hallway at the rear of the palace. The row of French doors leading to the garden beckoned. Tucking the album tighter under his arm, he turned and headed out into the night.

CHAPTER 12

AMANDA SWIPED AWAY THE LONE, hot tear burning a path down her cheek.

The entire diTalora family had been pitched into shocked mourning for Princess Lucrezia, and tomorrow the whole country would do the same. Amanda didn't have the luxury. The royal family had been extremely welcoming to her, but succumbing to her sadness over what they endured meant she'd never be able to do what she had to do.

She yanked open the top drawer of the marble-topped bureau, then pulled out her clothing and tossed it into a growing pile in her suitcase, no longer caring about keeping the items free of wrinkles or folded in any particular order.

Do not cry. Grab the socks. Do not cry!

She cleared the top of the bureau in one sweep, guiding her hairbrush and a mascara tube over the marble edge and into her already-jammed cosmetic bag.

As she fished her shoes from the floor of the armoire, images of the evening leaped unbidden into her mind. Marco's lean, muscular form causing heads to turn as he entered the ballroom with the bearing of a true prince. The look he shot her when he spoke with

Eliza Schipani. The unbridled thrill of success in his eyes as he distracted the barrel-chested Greek minister from a possible argument.

The hot, intimate kisses he'd given her in the library. The firm splay of his fingers along her breast before he swept his tongue across her nipple. The feel of his breath on her skin as he explored her body.

The look of rapture on his face before he entered her.

Heat rushed to her skin at the mere thought of that expression, followed by his mouth crashing down to meet hers. She paused and closed her eyes, remembering the feel of his hand easing between them, then the shiver when he found his release. The way he'd held her against him afterward, as both of them savored the phenomenon of what they'd shared.

She swore and slid her shoes into the suitcase's side pocket. No matter how intimate the moment, it couldn't cure Marco's questions. She understood the devastated look on his face when he realized what she'd been holding back from him, and his utter horror when Isabella's news proved how fragile life could be.

Amanda twisted her arm behind her back to unzip her evening gown, slipped the straps off her shoulders, then let the beading carry it to the floor. Habit compelled her to loop the hanging straps through the appropriate slots on the hanger that had come with the rich garment, but frustration caused her to stuff it in the armoire with less care than usual.

Satisfied she hadn't forgotten anything, she slipped into her most comfortable black pantsuit, then scribbled a quick note to Isabella, thanking her for the loaned suits she'd used in her first days at the palace and reiterating her sorrow over Lucrezia's death. She taped the note to one of the princess's outfits, which still hung in a neat row at one end of the armoire, then rang housekeeping to ask that a valet collect and return the princess's suits in the morning.

Isabella might need the black one for the events surrounding Lucrezia's funeral.

The princess had regained her composure soon after Marco left the library, at least enough to explain that Lucrezia had died of a burst aneurysm. Her death was completely out of the blue and the doctors had told Federico that even if he'd arrived at the hospital earlier, they likely couldn't have saved her.

Then Isabella had swept out of the room, intent on spending the night with Federico's now-motherless sons.

Amanda dropped her weary body onto the bed, sitting rather than lying down, for fear of falling asleep if she put her head on the pillow. Or worse, crying. As much as Lucrezia's sudden, tragic death saddened her, it was the stunned look on Marco's face when he'd demanded to know about her own health that caused hot tears to fill her eyes.

The last forty-eight hours had been an emotional roller coaster, and she hated herself for allowing it all to overwhelm her.

She ground her palms against her eyes, smearing bits of mascara onto her hands. Damn. Now she'd have to fix her makeup.

Focus. Focus. Focus.

She needed to get out of San Rimini.

Grasping the zipper of her suitcase, she pulled it around from back to front, swearing when a piece of material caught in the track. Instead of extracting the offending blouse, however, she jerked the zipper so hard it tore through.

She had to leave the palace tonight. Before King Eduardo could stop her. Before Marco could stop her.

In the moments before Isabella phoned, something had changed within Marco. Something in the way he felt about her. Up to that point, the entire evening could be summed up in one word: magic. They'd shared something meaningful, something that went well beyond sex.

Then she'd released her fears in an emotional outburst, telling him the one piece of information that would hurt him most. And from the look on his face, she knew her words washed away any chance for a future.

Hell, she'd said it herself. She might not have a future.

Her hands shook as she picked up her phone and connected to reservations for Air France. Much as she hated herself for sharing her medical history with him, it had been the right thing to do. If she and Marco were to pursue a romantic relationship, secrets couldn't linger between them, and this was a secret he couldn't handle. Not after he'd flat out told her about his own fears.

"Hello," she forced cheer into her voice when her call was connected through to an agent. "I'd like a spot on your first available flight from San Rimini to Washington, D.C. I could also go Venice to Washington, D.C. if there's nothing departing from San Rimini today. Do you have anything this morning?"

She listened for a moment, blinking to keep her tears under control. "Yes, of course I'll hold. Thanks for checking."

She hoped the agent couldn't hear her distress. She'd much rather have booked online, but the reservations window was closed for the morning flights. If there was space on one, she wanted to be on it, and that meant calling.

She paced the room as she waited, trying to sort through her jumbled emotions. Perhaps Marco could live with the knowledge she had a strong family history of breast cancer. He'd become more confident in himself since her arrival. He'd accepted his role in the royal family and learned for himself that he could stand on his own. In doing so, he'd started to overcome his fears of intimacy. He'd said as much in the library when he whispered to Amanda that she was worth the risk.

But how would Lucrezia's death affect him? Would seeing Federico's pain at losing a spouse so early in their marriage cause him to reconsider, if he hadn't already?

What would he think if she opted for preventative surgery? And if not, what would happen the day she discovered a lump in her breast? Heard that it was malignant? Or was diagnosed with *any* life-threatening illness, for that matter? After suffering the loss of his mother at a transitional time in his life—then watching Federico lose Lucrezia so abruptly—could she expect Marco to find the strength to help her through chemotherapy or radiation treatments, as her own father had helped her mom?

Or would Marco shut down, believing she would die and leave him alone again?

Amanda swallowed hard and stared at the ceiling. What a mess. She was thinking too much, and way, way too far into a nebulous future. All it did was upset her unnecessarily.

"Will you be traveling alone?"

She squeezed her eyes shut at the agent's question. "Yes."

"In that case, I can get you out this morning. We have a flight to Dulles airport connecting through Paris. It's full, but I believe I can get you on standby as there are a number of passengers who haven't confirmed. It leaves from San Rimini in three hours. Since it is an international flight, a two-hour advance check-in is required." The agent quoted a price, then asked what she wanted to do.

Amanda looked around the room that had become her home over the past few weeks. Leaving meant there'd be no chance of a future with Marco. None. For a split second, she wondered if she should wait and see what happened. Take a risk, see how he'd handle things once the events of the last forty-eight hours—and particularly the last eight hours—sank in and they could both get some perspective.

"Hello?"

You'll only hurt him in the long run.

"I can be at the airport in less than an hour." She gave the agent her payment and passenger information, noted the flight confirmation number, then ended the call.

Tonight, Marco had proven to himself that he could handle his royal responsibilities. He'd speculated that he didn't need her instruction anymore. Judging from how he handled tonight's dinner, he was right. At this point, he could teach himself through trial and error. If she stayed now, it'd only be for her own selfish purposes, and she couldn't do that to Marco after all he'd endured.

Women died on Marco diTalora. She didn't want to die on him, too.

MARCO SWORE ALOUD as the first rays of the morning sun struck the palace rose garden. He fingered a nearby leaf, wiping away the morning dew as Federico's words rumbled around in his brain.

He wasn't ready for a new day. Not yet.

He'd walked aimlessly through the rows of boxwood and roses after leaving Federico's room, allowing his heated emotions to cool. He'd just started to contemplate going inside and trying to get some sleep when he rounded a corner and found himself facing the arbor where he and Amanda had paused the night of Antony and Jennifer's wedding. Unable to bring himself to walk under the rose-covered arch, he turned and strode to a nearby bench, dropping into it with a thud.

For at least an hour, maybe two, he'd sat there, breathing in the cool air while his shirt gradually absorbed the dampness of the bench slats. All the while, the weight of the wedding album on his lap reminded him of his brother's words.

You have always been so certain you could avoid pain by avoiding love. It is not so.

And then the real kicker: *Not having love makes it worse.*

He loved Amanda. He knew it, as certainly as he knew anything in life. But loving Amanda might mean facing the pain of his mother's last days all over again.

Then again, he could spend the next few months or years in a wonderful relationship with her. Traveling together. Talking over the events of the day. Making love.

And on a sunny, summer afternoon, they could go to the Via Vespri for gelato and he could step in front of a tourist bus.

"Damn!" he muttered aloud.

"Your Highness? Is there something I can do to assist you?"

Marco started as Filippo approached him on the gravel path. He should have heard the driver's approach, but his mind had been too firmly wrapped around a certain brunette.

Filippo gave a quick bow. "I apologize if I startled you, Your Highness. I arrived early for my shift and thought I would come sit in the rose garden to drink my coffee." He raised a hefty travel mug. "I will leave you in peace."

"Have a seat, Filippo. I could use the company, if you don't mind."

A look of bewilderment crossed Filippo's face at the unusual request. "Of course, Your Highness. I am honored. Would you like me to get you some coffee first?"

"Last thing I need this morning."

Filippo nodded, then took the empty seat beside Marco.

"May I ask what you're holding?"

"Ah," Marco looked down, remembering the thick leather book. "Prince Federico's wedding album."

Filippo took a long sip of his coffee. "I heard the news when I arrived. You have my sympathy."

Marco shot his driver a half smile. "I appreciate that. I feel terrible for Federico and the boys. It won't be easy for them."

Filippo nodded his agreement.

The pair sat without speaking until a lone car rolled along the nearby garden drive, disturbing the silence as it made its way out the palace's rear gate. Normally, Marco would have been curious about the car and its occupant. No one left the palace so early, and most of the daytime staff wouldn't arrive for another hour or two. Even then, few had access to drive on that road. But with Lucrezia's death, there could be any number of doctors or members of Federico's staff keeping odd hours.

Filippo looked in the direction of the sound as well, then turned to Marco with a shrug. After a while, he asked, "Would you mind if I took a look at the album, Your Highness? I have never seen it."

Marco exhaled. "You know, Filippo, I haven't either. Federico gave it to me last night and told me I needed to see it."

Filippo raised one thick eyebrow. "Then perhaps now is a good time. Besides," he gestured toward the rear gate, "I only have twenty minutes before I am officially on duty."

Now that daylight had begun to kiss the treetops, Marco realized that Filippo wasn't the only one who'd pass through the garden.

He smoothed a palm over the top of the album. He'd put it off all night. Told himself there was no reason to look.

Now or never.

Marco flipped open the cover to reveal the first page. Then turned to the next. Filippo said nothing as Marco took his time, studying the familiar pictures one by one in the soft light of early morning, but seeing them with new eyes.

As the Duomo tolled the arrival of a new day, he gently turned the final page.

Leaning back against the cool bench, he closed his tired eyes, allowing the complex scents of the garden and the sound of the bells echoing off the hills to fill his senses.

As a child, while his father met with church officials, Marco had enjoyed tagging along to visit the Duomo and listen to the priests tell stories of the cathedral's past. He could picture the old bellman climbing the creaking wooden steps into the tower, double checking the clock's time against his own watch when he reached the lofty interior balcony, then pulling the ropes to toll the ancient bells.

Just as he did at every sunrise. Just as he did each Saturday night and twice on Sunday to call worshipers to the sanctuary. And just as he did to announce the celebration of a wedding.

The bench moved beneath him, causing Marco to open his eyes.

Filippo twisted the lid on his travel mug as he stood. "Thank you for sharing the album with me, Your Highness. The bells of the Duomo turn a man's mind inward, do they not?"

Marco kicked at the gravel beneath the bench, then eyed his driver. "Tell me, Filippo. How does a man with the skills of a Formula One race car driver also possess such wisdom?"

"I don't believe that is the mystery you should be pondering this morning, Prince Marco." Filippo pulled a wool driving cap from his pocket then placed it atop his head. "If you need me, I shall be at my station."

With that, the driver turned and strolled toward the rear gate, pausing briefly to tip his mug and capture its last drops, then replace the lid.

Still holding the image of the cathedral's peaceful gray interior in his mind's eye, Marco rose and stretched his legs, the muscles taut from his hours on the bench. Once he'd worked out the stiffness, he turned toward the palace, album tucked under his arm, and crunched through the gravel until he reached the arbor. Reaching out with his free hand, he touched one of the yellow roses overhead.

As he caressed the silken bloom, he knew what he had to do. Admitted to himself what he must have known, at some level, since the first time he'd kissed Amanda's hand and wrist, here under the arbor.

No woman had ever affected him as Amanda had. No matter what the risks, no matter what his fears, he couldn't have a relationship with a woman he couldn't love. Not only was it the coward's way out, it would eventually cause more pain than he'd ever known in his life.

And to lose Amanda…unthinkable. She filled his soul. He would fight any demon, face down any enemy—even death—if it meant sharing even one day of his life with her.

He found a protected spot under the arbor and set down Federico's album. He patted his pocket to ensure his Swiss Army knife hadn't fallen out when he'd kicked his pants off in his room earlier and was glad to feel the familiar hard edges. He withdrew it and cut the arbor's best blooms, carefully setting each stem in the gravel as he worked. When he had a dozen, he closed his knife, gathered the flowers and the album, then strode toward the palace kitchens.

"You're awake early."

Isabella startled him as he pushed open the door to the massive workspace. Despite the late night she'd had, she appeared pulled together as usual, sitting at one of the stainless steel counters on a stool often used by one of the chefs, and wearing her favorite coffee-colored suit. His sister looked him up and down, then gestured to his rumpled pants and tuxedo shirt. "Or perhaps you haven't slept at all."

"As the Americans say, bingo."

"I haven't, either." Isabella stretched to open the large bread warmer at the end of the counter and fished out a roll. She held it up. "Hungry?"

"Famished. But first I need to find a vase."

"I think there are a few under there," she inclined her head toward a large cabinet in the corner. He located a vase of clear Baccarat crystal with minimal decoration, perfectly suited to Amanda, and carried it to the sink. After filling it with water, he arranged the roses inside.

Satisfied, he turned toward his sister, caught the roll she threw at him, then took a bite.

"I don't suppose those are for Federico."

He leaned one hip against the counter, then swallowed. "No. But I plan to send him an arrangement later. And I'll have to think of something to do for the boys."

She stared at the flowers. "I see." Lowering her gaze, she cocked her head to the counter where he'd set Federico's album as he'd entered the kitchen and raised an eyebrow.

"Federico wanted me to hang onto it for a while. I don't think he could bear to look at it."

"He wanted *you* to look at it."

He took another bite of his roll, then met Isabella's knowing gaze. "Told you, did he? Can't anyone in this family keep a secret?"

Her mouth crooked into a half smile. "I saw him before he went to sleep. Right after you left him, I suppose." She sighed, her smile vanishing as they both ate their rolls and thought of Federico.

Isabella broke the silence first. "I think Federico's right. I'm not sure what was happening between you and Amanda when I interrupted you in the library last night. But you should know that she—"

"Amanda," he whispered. His mouth went dry and his stomach clenched as he stared at Isabella's suit. Why hadn't he realized it when he first entered the kitchen? Why hadn't Isabella said something the minute she saw him?

"She's gone." He said it as a statement, not a question. "That's one of the suits you lent her, isn't it?" The one Amanda had worn that first day in the library. He remembered how the rich brown shade made her hazel eyes stand out.

"It was hanging on my door this morning, along with the rest of the clothes she borrowed. All cleaned, with a note of thanks. She didn't say anything about leaving, though. Why would she? I thought Father hired her for three months."

Marco didn't hear the rest of Isabella's words. Leaving the flowers and the album behind, he shoved through the doors, nearly knocking over one of the cooks as she arrived for work. He called an apology over his shoulder, but continued walking purposefully through the dining room. When he hit the open hallway leading to Amanda's room, he broke into a sprint.

Finally, he faced her closed door. After pounding three times and hearing nothing from the other side, he tried the knob and found it unlocked.

"No," he whispered, his throat tightening as he surveyed the room.

Nothing. He knew this was where his Father arranged for her to stay, but there were no personal effects on the nightstand. No light coming from the adjacent bathroom. And no one in the bed. It hadn't been slept in.

Grabbing the phone off the nightstand, he punched in the three-digit code that would connect him to the guard station at the rear gate.

"This is Prince Marco," he said when a guard picked up, wishing he could get the words out fast enough to change what had already happened. "The car that left the palace early this morning. Was that Amanda Hutton?"

"*Si*, Your Highness."

"Was she headed to the airport?"

"I believe so."

A dozen choice expletives floated through Marco's mind at once, but he drummed them back. "Do you know what time her flight is?"

"I'm afraid not, Your Highness."

Damn.

"Call Filippo," he commanded. "Tell him I'll meet him at the gate. I want to be at the airport *pronto*." After slamming the phone back on the nightstand, he ran. Cold sweat dripped down his back by the time he reached the garden, then jogged past the fountain to the back gate.

He suspected no one, not even Filippo, could get him to the airport in time. It was his own stupid fault.

"Your Highness." Filippo urged Marco into the rear of the Range Rover, then wordlessly jumped into the front seat and stepped on the gas, throwing the prince against the back of his seat.

Marco strapped on his belt then closed his eyes so he wouldn't see how far they had to travel, or how many cars blocked their way.

All the years he'd spent in fear that a woman might die on him, afraid to get too close lest fate take a hand...what a waste. He didn't need fate to rip a woman from him, breaking his heart. He'd done it himself. His own paranoia and fear had driven away the perfect woman, breaking not one, but two hearts in the process.

"Your Highness?" Filippo ventured.

Marco opened his eyes and tried to keep his voice level. "Yes?"

"We shall be there in less than five minutes. I asked the other drivers...about Ms. Hutton, that is. She requested a driver take her to Air France for a flight to Paris. She mentioned that she was going on to Washington, D.C., so she wanted to be there early to check in."

"Do you know the time on the Paris flight?"

"I am sorry, no. But I checked while I was waiting for you. The first Air France flight to Paris doesn't leave for another forty-five minutes. Concourse C. It will board in twenty minutes. There's a second one twenty minutes after that on Concourse B. Both would arrive in Paris in time for a connection to Dulles airport in Washington, D.C."

Marco forced a smile to his face. "Thank you, Filippo."

He only hoped he could find her. And that he could find the words to convince her to stay.

CHAPTER 13

AMANDA STARED at the screen of her cell phone as she sat in the boarding area, trying to work up the courage to call home. Seven in the morning in San Rimini meant it was one a.m. in the District of Columbia, but odds were that her father, a perpetual night owl, hadn't yet retired. After finishing his paperwork for the day and ensuring her mother was asleep, he'd slip into his den to savor a nightcap, kick back in his leather recliner, and pick up the latest espionage thriller. Usually, he wasn't in bed for another hour or so.

Despite the good chance she'd catch her father in a quiet moment, she'd have been better off calling when she'd first arrived at the airport. All she'd done since then was agonize over what to say. In that time, nothing more profound than, "Hi, Dad. How's work? By the way, I walked out on the diTalora job, and no, I can't tell you why," came to mind.

She'd have to think of the right words during her flight. The clock was ticking. She'd hear from her parents when they woke in the morning and saw the news about Lucrezia. The palace wouldn't—couldn't—keep it quiet much longer. She didn't want her father trying to call while she was asleep somewhere over the Atlantic.

Amanda set her cell phone in her lap, then opened her wallet and discreetly thumbed through the bills.

When her plane landed in the United States, she'd only have one week before she'd need to either ante up the money for another month in her apartment or give notice and prepare to move in with her parents. Plus, she'd have to come up with the money to repay King Eduardo what she'd used to cover her current month's rent. Without completing the three months stipulated in their employment contract, she couldn't possibly keep the full salary he'd paid her in advance.

Converted to dollars, the cash she carried was enough to cover the late notice fee at her apartment and pick up her moving expenses. But not enough to repay the king.

She could already feel her father's sadness when she broached the subject of a loan. It wasn't that he wouldn't give her the money or that he'd tell her she hadn't lived up to his expectations. But he'd be let down all the same. She'd see it in his face and his body language. And she hated failing—again—to achieve all he'd hoped for her.

She closed her wallet and bit back a string of expletives, words she'd never used before she hunted down Marco diTalora in a casino and he'd turned her life upside down.

How had she let her feelings for him, someone so adventurous and unattainable, put her in this position?

Because you're in love with him.

"No," she chastised herself aloud, then forced a calmer expression when an elderly man in a nearby chair peered over his magazine at her.

Time to call Dad and hope for the best before she spent any more time thinking about it. She lifted the phone and was about to dial when a sign hanging from the concourse ceiling caught her eye.

Casino.

Her fingers froze. *No, don't.*

She wasn't a gambler. She'd played poker a few times during college and done well, and played slot machines and done not so well. Poker here would be nothing like poker with her friends. Her odds of winning enough to repay the king were slim, especially given the fact she'd only gambled a couple times in her whole life.

She certainly wasn't going to pull off a miracle like Marco's black-jack stunt.

I need to calm down before I make this call. No way did she want her father to hear her cry.

Amanda jammed the phone back into her handbag, deciding to make the call during her layover in Paris. Maybe, if she waited until just before she boarded her flight to the States, she'd catch her mother having breakfast. That would work.

She stood, shouldered her handbag, grabbed the handle of her suitcase, then followed the arrows to the down escalator.

Diversion. A diversion will help me calm down.

Within minutes, she crossed the threshold of the airport's semi-darkened casino. Lights flashed on electronic signs around the room tallying the current jackpots, and the lively ring of slot machines filled her ears.

Passengers lined up on stools, despite the early hour, watching the spinning symbols and nursing cocktails while they waited for their flights. A single roulette wheel spun along the wall to her left, behind a half dozen craps tables, only one of which was being used. To her right, a dozen blackjack tables formed a circle. The floor manager walked from table to table behind the dealers, taking notes on a clipboard.

Amanda eased onto a stool in front of a colorful slot machine billed as a Double Diamond.

"This one's lucky, right?" she asked the American-looking busi-nessman punching buttons on the machine next to hers.

"Hope it is for you, sugar." His drawl oozed pure Texas as he added, "I played it for half an hour, no luck. And this one's just as bad. I'm about to wipe out the last of what I put in it." The gray-haired man rubbed his hands together in front of his Lucky Sevens machine, closed his eyes, then gave the button a two-handed smack. The reels spun, then dropped into place for a loss.

"Ouch," Amanda said.

"I only bet what I can lose. Beats sitting at the gate, right?" He winked at her before moving down the row to a machine promising Easy Money.

Yeah, right. Easy for the casino.

She faced her own machine and tried to decipher the rows of diamonds, rubies, emeralds, and bars on the win chart. Betting a larger amount meant a bigger potential payoff, but beyond that the payouts didn't make much sense. Reaching into her wallet, she fished out a bill, then slid it into the appropriate spot.

"Here goes nothing." She waited for the money to register as credits, selected her bet, then touched the button on the front of the machine to spin the reels. As the diamonds and bars blurred before her, she envisioned Marco sitting behind her, cheering her on, but she quickly squelched the image. Gambling for a while before her flight was supposed to be a distraction from her problems, not a reminder.

The bars clicked to a stop one by one. Bar, double bar, zippo.

She studied the chart again, said a quick *come on* to the machine, then closed her eyes and hit the button again.

Double diamond. Double diamond. Double Bonus.

Bells sounded, then a light flashed on top of the machine as numbers indicating her win started to tally on the screen.

And they didn't stop.

The Texan jumped up from his Easy Money game. "Holy cow, sugar! I think you won back everything I put in that machine and a hell of a lot more. What multiplier did you bet?"

"Three," she told him. The maximum bet was five, so she'd gone for the middle ground. The clanging continued, and Amanda tried to decipher the payout chart. "I take it this is good?"

"Good? Naw. It's a travesty. You shoulda bet more." He leaned over her shoulder and pointed to one of the pictures on the chart. "Then you coulda had twenty-five hundred instead of fifteen hundred."

Amanda swallowed as the tally slowed and the ringing bells on top of the machine finally stopped. Sure enough, it told her she'd won fifteen hundred. Not a fortune, but when added to the sum in her wallet, it would pay back the king what she'd spent of her salary so far. It was a huge amount when balanced against the sum she'd bet.

She turned and smiled at the Texan. "I'm more than happy with fifteen hundred."

A petite blonde who Amanda guessed was around the same age as the Texan came around the end of the row of machines. "Hey, Al, was that you with the bells? Please tell me you hit the jackpot."

"Sorry, sweetie," he drawled. "This young lady just cleaned up. She won all the money I dropped in there, of course."

The blonde shot her a grin. "Good for you, honey."

Amanda hit the button to cash out, and the machine printed a receipt she could take to the redemption window. "Thanks. I hope your luck is just as good. Or better."

The blonde stuck out her lower lip. "Only if Al here will give me more money. Or we move on to blackjack and forget these silly slots."

"Sounds good to me, sweetie." He turned to Amanda. "I'm Al Stanmore, and this is my wife, Kristi. You're welcome to join us. We could use a good luck charm at our table."

Amanda introduced herself, but the blonde pouted at her husband. "What, I'm not a good luck charm?"

He shot Kristi the kind of look that told Amanda they were giddy in love and comfortable teasing each other. "You win anything yet?"

"No."

"Well, then."

Kristi grinned at Amanda, then angled a thumb over her shoulder, toward the far corner of the room. "Come on. You can tell us your life story over the blackjack table. We've heard all of each other's stories and could use some entertainment."

"Thanks for the invitation," Amanda said, then held up her receipt. "But I should cash out while I'm ahead. Besides, I'm flying standby and couldn't get on the first flight I wanted. I need to check in at the gate soon to see if they can fit me in on my second choice."

"Where are you headed?" Al asked.

"Paris, then D.C."

"Hey," Kristi smiled. "Us, too! Well, Paris to D.C. to Houston. Hate to tell you, but the flight's been delayed at least an hour. That's why we're in the casino."

"Mechanical problems," Al added, "or so they claim. But the woman working the gate told us there are four flights leaving Paris for Dulles this afternoon, and they all have available seats, so if we miss the connection, they'll be able to get us on another flight."

"That means you're stuck with us." The blonde pressed a couple of chips into Amanda's hand. "C'mon. We'll treat you to the first hand. What have you got to lose?"

Amanda glanced at the two red chips in her palm. She'd lost what was most valuable when she'd left the palace, so what harm could there be in losing a couple of chips? And gift chips, at that? She tipped her head toward the door leading to the concourses. "You're sure the flight's delayed? Air France 3422?"

"That's the one, sugar." Al laughed. "So whaddya say? You still on a hot streak?"

"I'm not sure one lucky pull on the slots counts as a streak." She looked from Al to Kristi, whose desire for female company was apparent on her face. "Oh, why not? But you're going to have to help me out. I've never really played."

Before she knew it, Amanda was parked to Kristi's left at a black-jack table. Al sat on Kristi's other side, flirting with his wife as if they were newlyweds. Another couple, Spanish, if Amanda had to guess, occupied the seats on the other side of Al.

The dealer shuffled the deck, then handed Kristi a thick yellow card and asked her to cut the cards.

"Not me," she said as Al gave her a peck on the cheek. "You can pass it to Amanda. She's the lucky one today."

Again, Amanda fought back the urge to tell them just how unlucky her last twenty-four hours had been. But she accepted the yellow card and cut the deck.

While the dealer loaded the cards into the shoe, Amanda made a discreet check of her phone to confirm that the flight was delayed. When she saw that Al and Kristi's information was accurate, she dropped it back into her bag, then asked Kristi, "Are you two on your honeymoon?"

Giggles erupted from Kristi and Al answered for her. "Naw. We just enjoy San Rimini. I came here on a business trip about twenty years ago and fell in love with the place. The beaches are spectacular, and you wouldn't believe—"

"Don't you dare tell her what we've done on those beaches, Al. We'd be arrested!"

Kristi turned to Amanda. "We make a point to come back every year now if we can afford it. We'd hoped to make it for the royal wedding, watch the carriage ride, all that. The whole story with Antony and Jennifer is so romantic, don't you think?" Amanda was thankful when Kristi continued without waiting for a response. "The airfares and hotel rooms were a lot cheaper after the wedding, though, so we decided to wait and come now."

"It looks like you had a good time."

Al snuggled up against Kristi. "You bet we did. Always do."

To Amanda's relief, the dealer called for the players to place their bets. Kristi and Al were wonderful people, but it was also tough to watch their romantic teasing.

Amanda stuck both of the chips Kristi had given her in the appropriate place on the green felt tabletop. Three hands later, she began to believe Al's prediction that she'd be lucky. She'd let each hand's winnings ride, and her two chips had multiplied to sixteen.

"Okay, I should quit now. Or at least bet less." Amanda reached for the growing stack, intending to remove all but two chips.

"No way," Al chastised her. "Those were free chips, young lady. Give yourself one more hand, then you can go redeem them."

"I'll at least give you back the two I started with—"

"Nope. You go for it."

Amanda took a deep breath. Winning four hands in a row was unthinkable. She couldn't believe she'd won three. After all, she knew as much about gambling as she did about investing in the stock market.

"Fine," she acquiesced. "But this is the last time."

"C'mon!" Kristi cheered as the dealer reached for the shoe to start a new hand. "Blackjack all around!"

The dealer began to lay the cards in front of them. A five and an eight for the Spanish couple. An ace for Al.

"You go, honey!" Kristi whooped.

A two for Kristi. She glared at the dealer. "Hey, I thought I said blackjack all around. What's that two?"

The dealer smiled at Kristi without commenting, then dealt a card to Amanda. A king.

On the second go round, Al got a queen for blackjack. Kristi landed an ace. "Well, that's something," she commented.

Then Amanda got another king for twenty. A good, solid hand, since the dealer now displayed a seven.

The feeling of déjà vu washed through her as she gazed down at the king of clubs and the king of spades. Just like Marco's hand that very first day they'd met, when he'd made his bet.

She'd thought him rash then, unpredictable. Irresponsible. The fancy pink dress and uncomfortable shoes she'd worn tramping from casino to casino in search of the missing royal had irritated her to no end.

But now she'd give anything to go back to that day and start over again, painful shoes and all.

The Spanish man hit until he went bust. His wife held at eighteen. Kristi hit to seventeen. Then the dealer turned to Amanda.

Just as she was about to swipe her hand over the cards to indicate she'd stay on twenty, something disturbed the air behind her, making the tiny hairs on the back of her neck prickle.

"Take a risk."

Everyone at the table turned to stare as Prince Marco reached over her and dropped a large bill on the table to cover the bet.

The dealer bobbed his head in respect. "Your Highness."

Amanda spun in her chair to face him, but the dealer interrupted, "The cards are still in play. What do you wish to do?"

Amanda's gaze met Marco's, then she turned back to the waiting dealer.

"Split them," she managed, though she hated to risk such a sum. The dealer couldn't hide his surprise at the wild bet, but he exchanged Marco's bill for chips as asked.

"What are you doing here?" Amanda whispered over her shoulder. "How'd you get through security without a ticket?"

"Looking for you, and I bought a ticket so I could get to the concourses without having to pull rank. Do you know how hard you are to track down?"

"I can guess. I seem to recall hunting all over San Rimini for you not too long ago."

"Touché." He placed his hands on the edge of the table, boxing her in. "Finish the hand. Then we'll talk."

Amanda tried to focus on the game in front of her, but her head was spinning. Marco had come to find her. Though he didn't seem angry, she wasn't certain whether his presence was good or bad. How could she possibly explain herself after walking out on him without a word?

The Spanish couple looked as if they were about to go into shock as they stared first at Prince Marco, then at Amanda, then back to Prince Marco. She couldn't blame them.

Kristi leaned over and whispered loud enough for Marco to hear, "Honey, you didn't tell me you know the royal family. And this is the cute one. No wonder you're so lucky!"

Amanda couldn't manage a response. Marco's arms rested on either side of her, muddling her senses. She inhaled sharply as the dealer separated her kings.

He drew a five for fifteen on the first hand, a two for twelve on the second.

Then he flipped his own card. An ace. Eighteen. As he scooped away her chips, Amanda's stomach lurched. What a time for her luck to run out.

"I should have known. Not the brightest bet." She turned to Al and Kristi. "I'm sorry."

"It's okay, honey, it was only two chips." Kristi patted her knee. "You've got more important things to handle." Kristi peered at Marco, her features making it clear she thought the loss of chips well worth seeing the prince up close.

"If you'll excuse us?" Marco asked, his gaze sweeping over everyone seated around the table. The dealer nodded and took a step back, giving them privacy while still keeping an eye on the chips. The Spanish couple practically fell over themselves vacating the area.

Al and Kristi got off their stools, but stayed within earshot, their curiosity winning out over decorum.

Marco didn't seem to care. He spun Amanda's stool so she faced him, then bracketed her by placing his palms on the table on either side of her. No one in the casino could miss the familiarity of his stance. "When I left the library last night, what were my last words to you?"

"I don't know," Amanda lied. She remembered every moment of the previous night.

"I said, 'This conversation's not over.' Now, before you do something stupid like hop on a plane home, let's finish our discussion."

"It's not important. Not anymore. And I shouldn't have said it the way I did—"

"It's damned important." Though he'd kept his voice quiet to dissuade eavesdroppers—including Al and Kristi—determination filled his eyes and a muscle twitched in his jaw. "Why was it so difficult to tell me?"

"Because I knew how it would affect you. I can see on your face that it upsets you to think about it now."

"Are you going to die?"

Her jaw dropped at his blunt question. "I hope not. Not anytime soon. But there are no guarantees."

"There are never guarantees. You could get hit by a car tomorrow."

"Gee, thanks."

"So could I." He was quiet for several long beats, while his expression remained serious. "From what I understand about breast cancer, having one or more genetic mutations doesn't mean a person automatically develops cancer. It means there's a higher chance."

"That's true. But it doesn't necessarily mean breast cancer. It could also mean ovarian cancer. And you said it yourself, after your mother's death—"

"We're not talking about her."

"But we are," she protested. She was careful to keep her voice low. "She's why you know what you do about the disease. You also saw what her death did to your father. You hated how it affected you. When you said that you wanted to see what the future holds for us—"

"I still do." His voice was quiet, certain.

"How?"

He took her hands in his. "Marry me. It's as simple as that."

Amanda's chest seized. She squeezed her eyes shut until she could steady herself.

Marry me. Could he really have said it?

"It doesn't have to be tomorrow," he said quietly. "It doesn't have to be a year from now. But I want you to stay here, in San Rimini, and I want us to be together. I want it to be with an eye toward forever, or as long as forever can be. I love you, and probably did from the moment you dragged me out of the casino and refused to put up with my attitude."

"I love you, too, Marco. That's why I felt I needed to leave this morning." She managed to meet his gaze. She wanted him to see everything she felt and how deeply she felt it. "But...there's so much we don't know about each other."

"Then we'll take our time and learn. I can't think of anything I'd rather do. I already know what's most important. You're capable, you're funny, you're the sexiest woman I've met in my life, and you believe in me, even when I have my doubts. You're kind and respectful to everyone you meet. I saw it in the way you thanked Filippo when he drove us to the Duomo and in the care you showed my sister last night." His hands came off the table to capture hers. "Stay. Stay forever."

Her throat clogged, a precursor to tears. She sucked in a breath, which only made her jaw shake. On a laugh, she said. "Did you know I'm five years older than you are? When you're thirty-five, I'll be forty. And when you're forty-five, I'll be fifty. *Fifty.*"

He shrugged. "So what?"

"Excuse me, Your Highness," Al said, taking a timid step toward them, "you're proposin' marriage, and you don't even know the lady well enough to know her age?"

"Proper etiquette dictates that a man never ask a woman her age." Marco winked at Amanda before adding, "However, if she chooses to reveal it, it's fair to tell her she looks gorgeous no matter the number."

"Marry him now!" Kristi urged.

"I have no idea who these two are," he said, sparing the couple a quick sideways glance. "But you should listen to them. Marry me. Please."

"Are you sure, Marco?"

"That's not what you're supposed to be say, just say yes!" Kristi's words would have made Amanda laugh if the look on Marco's face wasn't so deadly serious.

His gaze bored into her. "I've urged you to take more risks. Stop being so cautious."

"It's prudent to think things through and plan ahead. That's why I do the job I do."

"Perhaps. But from the moment we met, you've taken risks. Barging into the private gaming room. Accepting my father's job offer, then convincing me I could handle an important dinner. And most of all, you risked your career, walking out on a job because you didn't want to hurt me."

"I still don't want to hurt you."

He shook his head. "No one can completely avoid pain in life. But it's a lot easier to face when you have love."

He dropped to his knee on the red carpet of the casino floor, in front of Kristi and Al and a growing crowd. "I'll ask you a third time. Amanda Hutton, will you marry me? I love you. You're worth any risk. And I know this isn't the proper way to propose, without a ring or anything, but if you say yes, I'll remedy that as soon as possible."

Her heart nearly burst at the sight of his earnest face and the adoration she saw there. In a whisper, she replied, "The only requirements for a proper proposal are for one party to ask and the other party to respond, hopefully in the affirmative."

His eyes flickered in hope. "I've done my part. Do you have a response?"

She smiled, wanting to savor the moment and the realization that if Marco diTalora was able to overcome his fear of crowds and propose to her in front of hundreds of strangers in a very public place, he could overcome anything.

If he could, so could she.

She bent. A breath before her lips met his, she said, "Yes."

EPILOGUE

"A LIMOUSINE WOULD HAVE BEEN MORE appropriate, you know. Or the carriage King Eduardo offered." Amanda's father glanced at the mound of white fabric bunched in her lap. "This car was not designed for a wedding gown."

Amanda fluffed the dress, then grinned. "A very wise person once told me 'the hell with appropriate.' I think that was good advice. At least in regard to my transportation today."

She ignored her father's shocked look and smiled out the window of Marco's black Range Rover as it crept along the Strada il Teatro. Through the open window, she waved to the toddlers held high on their parents' shoulders and at a group of university students jumping up and down on the wide sidewalk screaming her name and wishing her good luck. She smiled at the older children crouched low at the front of the crowd so they could wave San Riminian and American flags through the traffic barriers. A policeman on horseback tipped his hat in greeting as she passed, and she could swear he had tears in his eyes.

"Besides," she added as they rounded the corner leading uphill to the Duomo, "there will be plenty of time for appropriate once we reach the cathedral."

"True." Her father patted her knee, or attempted to, given that it was hidden under a pile of silk. A moment later, he said, "This is a big step, and it's both a public and a private one. But I know it's what you want, and I'm glad you reached out and grabbed that destiny with both hands. I'm so proud of you, honey, for so many reasons. You and Prince Marco will be happy together for many, many years."

"I know." And she should have known all along. Both of her parents loved her. Any fears she would let them down came from within herself. It was something she and Marco had learned from each other over the course of their engagement. So much fear—both fear of failure and fear of success—came from within. It wasn't rooted in reality.

They'd attended more public events together than she could count, everything from a climate summit in Switzerland to school visits throughout San Rimini. Marco had planned and hosted a number of events as well, including a two-day long music festival, with all the proceeds going to support patients in the wing of Royal Memorial Hospital that was dedicated to his mother.

They had shared private moments, too. Lucrezia's funeral was the low point, though in some ways, it made Marco and Amanda value every moment they had together. The high point was a hiking trip through rural Cambodia, which had been an adventure. Marco had encouraged her to try things she never thought she could do, like ride on the back of an elephant as it waded across a river, eat foods she couldn't identify, and take side trails that required they navigate rough terrain. In each case, she'd learned something new and expanded what she'd believed were her limits.

She and Marco were a good balance for each other.

On top of all that, by the end of the day, Jennifer would be her sister-in-law.

To no one's surprise, Jennifer had been thrilled by news of the engagement. Within hours of hearing about the airport proposal, Jennifer had made a standing monthly reservation for the back room of her favorite local restaurant, explaining to Amanda that with both of them now living in at the palace, they needed a regular girls' night out.

Those evenings had been a joy. On their last outing, they'd invited Princess Isabella to join them. Though the princess had been quiet at first, she eventually relaxed, and the three of them spent an evening filled with laughter and shared stories of the near disasters they'd each had during public appearances.

Amanda suspected the princess needed to escape the scrutiny of palace life more often.

Amanda's father grinned and waved out his window as a little boy clutching a balloon waved at the Range Rover. "You never told me. Did you decide to use traditional wedding vows or write your own? I know you'd planned to discuss it with the king, but it wasn't covered during the rehearsal yesterday. The priest simply mentioned when the vows would occur in the ceremony."

"Actually, neither. We've decided to wing it. With the king's and the priest's permission, of course."

Her father leaned back against the seat and stared at her. "You must be joking. I'm surprised the king would allow it."

She reached over to pick a piece of white lint off her father's slacks, remembering how Marco had reached across the vehicle's wide back seat to fix her dress the day they'd met.

"It'll be fine, Dad," she reassured him. "We love each other. We figured we'd simply say what was in our hearts when we get there. That would make it more memorable, and more meaningful, for both of us."

"Your wedding is being broadcast around the world. You aren't worried you or Marco will say something embarrassing?"

She laughed as they pulled in to the wide circular drive in front of the Duomo. As the bells tolled her arrival, a group of San Riminian soldiers in ceremonial garb formed lines on either side of the staircase in preparation for her father to walk her inside.

"We won't," she assured her father. "And even if we do, we decided it would be worth the risk."

She kissed him on the cheek, then waited as he exited the Range Rover, then walked around the vehicle to open her door.

She couldn't wait to take the next step.

Thank you for reading *The Prince's Tutor*. If you enjoyed this book, please consider leaving a review at your favorite bookstore or book club website.

Learn about Nicole's upcoming releases and receive special insider bonuses by subscribing to her newsletter at nicoleburnham.com.

Read on for an excerpt from the next San Rimini novel, *The Knight's Kiss*.

THE KNIGHT'S KISS

Prologue

San Rimini, November 1190

Two men he could defeat. Perhaps three, given the element of surprise.

But from his hiding place behind a tangle of low bushes, deep in the richly forested hill country of San Rimini's western borderlands, Domenico of Bollazio counted five men in the glade. Turkish spies, he realized with alarm, noting they wore San Riminian garb yet spoke with heavy accents and carried Turkish short swords. They stood in a circle, kicking angrily at a whisper-thin youth of no more than fifteen years.

A fool's mission, Domenico warned himself, reluctantly drawing his fingers away from the leather-padded grip of his own sheathed sword. Better to ignore his instinct to help the lad and return to his horse to complete his real mission.

Even so, he couldn't help but watch as the youth on the ground cried out in Italian, begging for mercy. The infidels paid him no heed. They'd come for blood and no doubt they'd have it.

"Where is it?" one of the armed men demanded. His accent made him difficult to understand, but there was no mistaking the threat in his tone. "Make it easier on yourself and tell us now where you have hidden it." He kicked the young man in the ribs for emphasis.

Domenico closed his eyes at the sickening sound of bones breaking. Cursing himself for stopping, for allowing himself to care, he eased away from the edge of the glade, careful not to rustle the thick coat of autumn leaves beneath him.

"I know nothing of this...this message!" The young man's frightened cry carried to Domenico's ears despite the knight's determination to shut out the sound.

"Deny it if you wish. Our spies know the king's messenger was to pass here this morn on his way to Messina."

Domenico stilled, his heart turning to ice in his chest. Crouched low, he crept back to the glade, his attention riveted on the scene unfolding before him.

"Do not let him leave," one of the infidels ordered the rest, keeping to Italian so the youth would understand his words. "If he continues to foolishly insist on his innocence, do with him as you please, then search the area. It's likely in the woods nearby."

Out of habit, Domenico's hand rubbed the pommel of his sword. In his gut, however, he knew any rescue attempt would be futile. The young man rolled on the ground and attempted to gain his feet, but stopped when the tallest of the Turks drove a dagger into his leg.

Anger rose in Domenico's chest, but he had no time to contemplate the innocent youth's injury or his death, which would likely come soon. Afterward, the spies would discover what Domenico had, that the youth's pack pony carried only a half day's provisions. He hadn't the means to convey a message to the other side of the peninsula over difficult terrain.

But if Domenico didn't make his own escape now, the men would certainly find *him*, and perhaps even the message they sought, now safely tucked against his chest, sewn into the lining of his quilted gambeson.

King Bernardo had warned Domenico of the importance of the

message, and that there were those who would give their life to see its contents. Less than two hours after he'd left the San Riminian king's presence, the knight realized the truth of those parting words. He'd be lucky to reach Lionheart and his army, now camped with France's Philip Augustus on the island of Sicily, alive.

Within minutes, Domenico located his horse, hidden amongst the trees a short distance from the glade. He guided the animal to the road, but before he could mount, a noise in the nearby bushes startled him. He spun around just in time to see a panicked woman with fiery red hair pick her way out of the brush.

"Please, my knight," the woman begged, approaching without hesitation to grab his arm, "have you seen a young man about? Fourteen years of age, with hair the color of fresh straw?"

The youth. Domenico glanced over his shoulder, ensuring the woman's voice hadn't alerted the soldiers to his presence. When he was certain they hadn't been heard, he turned his attention back to her. Judging from her age and the desperate look on her face, he suspected she might be the poor lad's mother. Still, that wasn't what set his nerve endings abuzz in warning. There was a familiarity to the woman, though Domenico knew he'd never laid eyes on her in his life.

Keeping his voice soft, he asked, "What is your name, madam? How do you come to be near the border? Do you not realize how dangerous—"

"They call me Rufina. Please, I know you have seen my Ignacio. Your eyes tell me so."

Rufina the Witch?

No wonder she seemed familiar. He'd heard of the red-haired conjurer who lived in this area, a woman who'd been fortunate enough to flee the city before being tried for her crimes against the church.

Though he did not believe in witchcraft himself, Domenico sensed brushing her aside would be a mistake. "I have seen him. Over yon, in the glade. But he is in trouble—"

Not bothering to ask what kind of trouble, the woman turned in the direction Domenico pointed. Before she could take two steps, he grabbed one of her bony elbows. "A group of infidels have captured him. If you enter the glade, they will likely kill you. Wait until they are gone and you will be able to treat the young man's wounds. 'Tis your best hope."

Rufina was known to be practiced in the healing arts, though the pious accused her of calling on the Devil himself for assistance. With her skills, the youth might have a fighting chance at life.

If he wasn't dead already.

Rufina didn't appear to find the advice helpful, however. She stared at Domenico, her eyes filled with a hate and blame as complete as that of any warrior he'd faced in battle. "My son is bodily injured, yet you do nothing? How dare you wear that sword and call yourself a knight of San Rimini!"

She raised her hand to strike him, but Domenico moved faster, corralling her thin wrist midswing. "I could not. I am on a mission from the king, and to assist your son would have jeopardized it." He swore to himself and dropped her wrist. He shouldn't have revealed so much. "Please understand, madam. Go now, do what's best to help him—"

"Mission for the king," she spat, showing no fear. "You possess a knight's sword, yet you wear no crest of nobility. Is the king's mission so pressing you cannot stop to help someone in need? A young man raised in a humble home, as you were? Or is it your ambition—ambition to gain your own lands and title by currying the king's favor—that prevents you from taking even the slightest risk to help another?"

Domenico started in surprise. In only a few sentences, this woman —this witch—summed up his life better than he could himself. He didn't care for her conclusions.

His horse shuffled beside him, reminding him of his purpose. "I must go. You would be well advised to—"

"Oh, I shall save him, never you fear. And your guilty conscience. But know this" —she shoved her hand deep into the folds of her dirty woolen tunic— "until you can abandon your ambition and sacrifice your own desires for the sake of another, you will know neither the true happiness of this world nor the peace of death. You value your life so much you refuse to risk it? Then life you shall have!"

She withdrew her hand from her tunic in a flash of motion. Domenico sidestepped, expecting her to brandish a dagger of the type unsavory women often wore for protection, but instead her palm held only a green powder, which she flung in his face. Annoying prickles of fire stung his cheeks as he swiped it away. Probably concocted of poison ivy or some such plant.

Voices rose in anger in the distance, distracting him from the conjurer's efforts to cow him. This foolish woman would get him killed.

"Secrete yourself, madam!" he hissed, then swung his leg up and over his horse. Turning toward Venice and the long road to Sicily beyond, Domenico made a fervent wish to never again cross paths with Rufina.

ALSO BY NICOLE BURNHAM

ROYAL SCANDALS

Christmas With a Prince (prequel novella)

Scandal With a Prince

Honeymoon With a Prince

Christmas on the Royal Yacht (novella)

Slow Tango With a Prince

The Royal Bastard

Christmas With a Palace Thief (novella)

The Wicked Prince

One Man's Princess

ROYAL SCANDALS: SAN RIMINI

Fit for a Queen

Going to the Castle

The Prince's Tutor

The Knight's Kiss

Falling for Prince Federico

To Kiss a King

BOWEN, NEBRASKA

The Bowen Bride

A ROYAL SCANDALS WEDDING

More Royal Scandals titles will be available soon. For updates, please visit nicoleburnham.com, where you can subscribe to Nicole's Newsletter.

Subscribers receive exclusive content, including the short story *A Royal Scandals Wedding*, an inside look at the wedding of Megan Hallberg and Prince Stefano Barrali from the novel Scandal With a Prince.

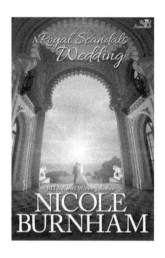